With A *Bite*

5 Vampire Tales

Rebecca M. Senese

Other Books by Rebecca M. Senese

The Night Killers

The Colour of Blood: The Chronicles of Richard Damon

Oh the Horror! 5 Horror Stories

Wreck the Halls: 5 Christmas Horror Stories

Who Killed Santa? A Christmas / Mystery Novella

A Very Zombie Christmas

The Beginners Guide to the Recently Deceased

Bad Ends: 5 Horror Stories

By Howl & Claw: 5 Werewolf Stories

Life Among the Dead: 5 Zombie Stories

Zombie Safari

The In-Between Series
Book 1: A Reluctance of Blood
Book 2: A Remembrance of Flesh
*Book 3: A Retribution of Soul

*Forthcoming

With A *Bite*

5 Vampire Tales

Rebecca M. Senese

RFAR Publishing
Toronto, Canada

Published 2014 by RFAR Publishing
Toronto, Canada
http://www.RFARPublishing.com

With a Bite: 5 Vampire Tales © 2014 Rebecca M. Senese. All rights reserved. No part of this book may be used, transmitted or reproduced in any form or by any means, electronic or mechanical, including photocopying, recording or by any information storage and retrieval system, without written permission except in the case of brief quotations embodied in critical articles and reviews. For more information, contact Rebecca M. Senese: rms@RebeccaSenese.com

This is a work of fiction. All characters appearing in this work are fictitious. Any resemblance to real persons, living or dear is purely coincidental.

Trade paper edition designed by Rebecca M. Senese
in InDesign CS5.5

Electronic editions designed by Rebecca M. Senese

Cover design: Rebecca M. Senese
Cover Image © nulus / SXC.hu
Interior Image © S-E-R-G-O / DepositPhotos.com
Xelissa / DepositPhotos.com

ISBN: 978-1-927603-28-4

Publications Acknowledgement

"Hard Body." First published in *Hungur Magazine,* 2011.

"Returning Home." First published in *The Vampire's Crypt,* 1998.

With A

Bite

5 Vampire Tales

TABLE OF CONTENTS

Introduction......................................1

Returning Home.............................5

Hard Body......................................31

Back in the Day.............................61

Bloody Aversion...........................83

The Whitest Smile.......................125

INTRODUCTION

Welcome to my collection of vampire stories.

Vampires are an interesting mix of power and weakness. During the night, they are unstoppable, but during the day, they are helpless.

And then there's that whole blood thing.

So what is it about vampires that is so interesting? I think it's the ability to shed the old life and become something new, something powerful, something dangerous, something that lives outside the rules. But what happens when the world catches up, and vampires have to live by the rules? One of my vampires finds out. Or what do you do when your normal human frailties impacts your ability to feed. Another of my vampires finds that out.

And where does a vampire go for good dental hygiene? I would think that would especially important for any vampire.

I think of vampires this way, in an odd sort of sideways direction. Seems a lot of my stories go like that, kind of weird.

So why should my vampires be any different?

Enjoy!

Rebecca M. Senese
December 2013

Returning Home

The naked bulb of the basement light stung her eyes as Katherine Snelman clutched the slim piece of paper in her hands. The postmark on the envelope read September of the year before, seven months before her mother's death. It seemed impossible, her mother had never told her about this letter, had never hardly mentioned her father, yet the proof was in her trembling hands.

"My dearest Angela,

Although it has been over thirty years since I last saw you, I think of you often. For so long I have respected your wishes, allowed you to live the life you wanted, now I ask that I be allowed to become a part of it again.
Remember how we danced at the Wonderland Gardens? The sweet smell of roses still brings your face to my mind. I know you must think of me and wonder. Wonder no more!
I will be on the footbridge to the park at midnight on the seventh. I would like to see you, even if only to see you. Please come.

Daniel"

Her hand shook as she brushed the mousy brown bangs out of her eyes. She'd been slowly sorting through her mother's correspondence the past three months, living and reliving the last painful months, the many weekends she'd spent on the road from Toronto to London, visiting her mother, watching as she slipped ever farther away. Her mother had always been proud, even toward the end, refusing hospitalization and arguing with the doctors. Tears stung Katherine's eyes; so typical of her.

Had she gone to meet him, she wondered. At midnight, for god's sake! The footbridge was at least a mile away on the far end of the golf course. On this side of the river it sat at the end of a steep, tree lined road that branched to the footbridge one way and the golf course another. On the other side of the river was Springbank Park, a beautiful rolling park of trees and grass and flowers. But closer to the footbridge, the park gave way to more wild growth of dense underbrush and gnarly trees.

Oh, this was ridiculous, she was getting all worried and upset as if her mother could get hurt now. This was a letter from the past, albeit a strange one. Her mother had probably kept it out of sentiment, not telling her because she knew it would only hurt Katherine; being reminded of a father who had abandoned them. God knows at her age her mother wouldn't have gone down there.

She wanted to throw out the letter, but her hand, having a mind of its own, placed it on a stack of boxes beside the garbage bag. She picked up the shoe box, determined to forget about the letter, and continued to sort through the papers. Bills and more bills. Invitations to join the Book-of-the-Month club. Requests from Save the Children. She tossed it all.

Occasionally her hand brushed the letter. By accident. Her eyes flicked over to see it, to ensure its reality. The paper lay on the boxes, slightly wrinkled. An innocent timebomb.

Suddenly she had to go there, to stand where her father had stood, waiting for her mother. Had he leaned against the rusting rail, green paint dulled by the sun, flaking beneath his elbow? What had he looked like? His features probably would have been as hard to discern in the moonlight as in the old faded picture her mother had kept.

Katherine set the shoe box down beside the garbage bag and picked up the letter. She brushed her fingertips lightly across the signature. Daniel. An elegant sounding name, not blunt and hard like the short form Dan.

She left the basement light on and the door open. Pausing in the front hall, she slipped on her sandals and considered a light jacket. After such a hot day she wouldn't need it. She stuffed the keys in her pocket and turned on the outside light. The door locked behind her but she giggled the knob just to be sure.

The night was still warm, comfortable after the scorching summer day. The grass beneath her feet felt lush and springy. A thunderstorm two days ago had brought it back from a dried yellowing state.

Katherine reached the road and looked across. The golf course lay shrouded in darkness, but she knew the far end dipped toward the river. The road was empty of traffic. Katherine crossed and walked along the edge of the golf course, following the fence.

The sound of crickets reached her ears and she marveled. She'd never heard such natural sounds in Toronto. She'd forgotten how peaceful it could feel. The crickets seemed to lead her on, along to the end of the golf course.

She turned right, following a new road as it dipped down toward the river. For a short while it followed the golf course then veered off into a sharp decline. Shapeless maples rose in the darkness on both sides of the road, crowding out any possibility of sidewalks. The streetlights were few here, spaced far apart.

Katherine slowed as she followed the decline. She could feel the paper in her hand, hear its soft crackle in the light breeze. The leaves of the maples rustled in response, a secret code she could not understand. She felt suddenly chilly but the breeze was not that cold.

What was she doing here, had she gone completely mad? It was after midnight and here she was walking alone in a badly lit area, too far from any houses. She would never have done this in Toronto. She'd let London's familiarity dull her senses. This was no longer the town of her childhood with the neighbourhoods where everyone knew each other and children played confidently in the parks, unmolested by drug dealers or stalkers. London was no longer immune to muggers stalking the streets. She'd been lucky to get this far.

Just turn around and walk back, keeping a brisk pace, she told herself. No need to panic. She turned. The breeze made the letter in her hand crackle.

She would come tomorrow in the daylight, when it was safe, when it was sane. It made more sense, a smart practical decision. Why did it make her feel so hollow?

She glanced back over her shoulder, down the road that led into a pool of darkness at the bottom. Her eyes adjusted sufficiently to the dark to discern the general shape of the road. The breeze sent her short, mousy brown hair dancing on her forehead. It wouldn't be the same in the daylight, she realized. She wouldn't be able to fully imagine her father, to really feel him. And her mother.

Reluctantly she turned and began to follow the road down. At least she told herself she was reluctant, she told herself that her quickening steps were only the results of the steepness of the decline. Her heart pounded only from the exertion. She clutched the letter only because she didn't want it to fly away in the breeze.

By the time she reached the bottom of the hill she was running. The road forked, branching one way toward the golf club house, a large hulking shape barely visible around the bend. Branching the other way, the road turned down toward the river, toward the footbridge.

She turned left toward the footbridge. The path narrowed further. The trees, with branches hanging low, pressed closer to the road, making her feel almost claustrophobic. The asphalt quickly turned to gravel, continuing to narrow until it was barely two people wide. The vegetation on either side seemed ready to engulf the road at any instant, swallowing her whole as well. The smell of the leaves was sharp in her nostrils, making her feel heady. She realized she'd missed this natural wildness in Toronto, too much concrete and safe, contained parks with manicured lawns and sculpted trees.

Suddenly the footbridge loomed up ahead of her, metal steps leading up to the wooden floor. Rusting girders defined the structure. She remembered the times the city had condemned the bridge and vowed to tear it down. They'd even seal off the entrances but kids would inevitably climb over the barriers and the city was forced to restore the bridge to ensure safety. Once she'd even done it herself, coaxed on by Benny Richmond, his freckled face flushed with excitement above her, his hand reaching out to her. At eleven it had been the thrill of a lifetime, to have Benny Richmond reaching for her hand.

Katherine took a hold of the railing and began to climb.

The metal was cool beneath her hand. All the paint had worn off, leaving a smooth surface. The stairs whined slightly beneath her feet. Another step up and she was on the walkway.

It stretched on forever. The other side was a distant darker smudge on black. Although she couldn't see much of the bridge she felt the suggestion of its form. The beams shot high into the air, arching downward elegantly. Strong cables, invisible in the darkness, tethered the bridge to the land. Katherine didn't need to see them, she remembered watching birds sitting on the cables, swaying in the breeze.

Had her father come onto the bridge from this side or the park side? Had he lingered at one end, or made his way out to the centre? He would walk to the centre, she decided. There was no reason for her to think that but she liked the idea.

Again she took a hold of the rail and allowed it to lead her toward the centre of the bridge. The water of the Thames, a dark polluted green during the daytime, was now black, an invisible gurgling carpet. The sound of it, an ever present background noise, took centre stage, growing louder as she traveled away from the land.

Finally she reached the centre and stopped, waiting for the sway of the bridge to finish. She remembered racing with Benny Richmond across the walkway, just to feel the sway. Or they'd jump up and down, then stand still. It was like being able to shake the world.

She laughed out loud, her voice trickling off into the distance. Crickets chirped a response. She loved it here, felt free from everything.

Had he stood at this spot, she wondered. Leaning against the rail, did he smoke a cigarette, tapping off the ash to watch it fall lazily into the water. Daniel.

She imagined her mother coming to meet him. She would have worn a white dress, easier for him to see her. He'd call out to her when she appeared, guiding her with his voice. She'd advance slowly, carefully feeling her way until they stood together. He would have brought her a rose.

Katherine became aware of the tears on her cheeks and she chuckled to herself. What an idiot she was, daydreaming romance for her poor dead mother. Maybe she'd wanted a father more than she realized. It wouldn't make any difference now. For all intents and purposes, she was alone.

As she began to walk back across the bridge a breeze rose up, ruffling her hair. She pushed the bangs out of her eyes and took another step. Her foot missed then slapped on the wood. The bridge was swaying in the breeze, faster than before.

Katherine slowly became aware of her position. The bridge was old, the flooring made up of wooden planks, many probably ready to fall through. She could be plunged into the swift current of the river. What the hell was she thinking?

Get off, she told herself. She grabbed the rail and began sliding her feet forward. Her hair danced around her face, darting in and out of her mouth. The breeze whistled in her ears, making tones, distorting, twisting the crickets and nights sounds into a voice.

Calling her.

Katherine stopped and looked around. The darkness felt thick and heavy. The breeze was cold but sweat trickled down her fleshy sides. Her mouth was dry as she tried to swallow. The breeze lulled, then picked up again.

"Katherine..."

There, she'd heard it. The paper crackled in her hand as she clenched it. The sound made her jump. The bridge swayed a little more beneath her feet.

Someone else was on the bridge.

Never mind it was irrational, or she'd have heard anyone approaching in the stillness, she knew someone was there.

She had to get off the bridge.

She turned around and realized she didn't know which way she was facing. Was it the park in front of her or behind? How many times had she turned? Had she been facing the right way in the first place? Where was the person who was on the bridge with her?

The breeze brushed her arms and she shivered. Goose pimples formed on her arms and beneath her t-shirt. The jeans felt clammy and tight on her legs. She wanted to scream but her throat was so dry she feared it wouldn't make a sound.

"Katherine."

A man's voice spoke from behind her. She gripped the railing until her fingers hurt. She felt colder, much colder than she had any right to feel on this warm evening. She wasn't going to turn around, wasn't going to look. But her head moved of its own volition, turning slowly to the left.

For a moment she expected -- Benny Richmond -- as her mind reached for something to steady her. She could actually see his freckled face and red crewcut before the image faded, turning into...

A man.

He was tall and thin, wearing dark pants and a lighter shirt, the colours hard to discern in the darkness. His skin was white, shining out of the cuffs and neck of his shirt like a beacon. One thin white hand touched the railing. The other brought a cigarette up to his pale lips. The tip flared bright red as he took a drag.

Smoke obscured his face as he released it through his flaring nostrils. When it dissipated she saw he had a proud, aquiline nose and wide blue eyes. A slight smile touched his lips.

"I had no idea you'd come here, Katherine." His voice was a deep rumble, low in his chest.

Katherine shifted a little to face him. How had he snuck up behind her so silently? Why hadn't she smelled his cigarette? She was allergic to smoke and could smell it coming a block away, even outside.

Stall him, keep him talking.

"How do you know my name?" she asked.

"Your mother's told me all about you. She's very proud."

Katherine stiffened. Who was this man to talk about her mother? Anger tinged the edges of her fear, giving her strength.

"Who are you?" she demanded. "What are you doing here, following a woman around in the dark. I could have you arrested!"

He chuckled. "You do have spirit, just like she said. Good to see it." He took another drag on his cigarette, letting the smoke out slowly, watching her with such obvious amusement that her anger swept away her fear.

Then his face slowly lost its humour, becoming more serious. "Don't you know?" he asked. "I thought you'd guessed, that's why you came here."

"Guessed what?" She spoke a little more reticently. His seriousness dispelled her anger, allowing her fear to return.

"I'm your father," he said.

The fear returned in full bloom. Cold sweat trickled down her back. He was a madman, she thought, and she was standing in the middle of a river with him.

"I thought you'd guessed," he repeated. "I did everything she asked. Left you both alone until you'd grown up and moved away. I gave her seven months to straighten everything up, to give you time to get used to her death. I could have taken her in one night but she thought it would be too much of a shock for you."

Katherine stared at him. Was he the one who was mad? She was beginning to wonder. He looked no older than thirty-five. Mousy brown hair ruffled across his forehead in the breeze and he brushed it back with an impatient gesture.

Mousy brown.

Her mother'd had black hair, before it had gone grey. She'd always told Katherine she had her father's hair. Mousy brown.

She stared at him, unable to think of anything to say.

"Daniel, what are you doing?"

Katherine spun at the sound of the voice behind her. A strangled cry gurgled from her throat. She made a grab for the railing as her knees buckled. Her hand missed and she fell to her knees, setting the bridge swaying again.

Her mother stood before her, wearing the cream dress she'd worn in her casket. Her hair hung down to her shoulders and looked almost black. Her face, white even against the light cream of the dress, looked less wrinkled. Katherine's mouth dropped open as tears filled her eyes.

"Oh look what you've done, Daniel," her mother said. "You've upset her."

"We were doing fine, Angela." He sounded hurt. "I thought maybe you'd told her."

"Why would I tell her, for god's sake." Her mother slapped the railing for emphasis in a familiar gesture.

I am crazy, Katherine thought, dazed.

Angela bent down and took Katherine's shoulders. "I know this is a shock, darling, and I'm sorry. What are you doing here?"

"Letter," Katherine managed to croak out of her uncooperative mouth. She glanced at the wadded paper in her hand.

Gently her mother extracted the paper from her fingers. As she smoothed it out, Katherine wondered at the coldness of her touch.

Angela stood after she read the letter, folding it carefully in half. "Oh dear," she said to Daniel. "She found the letter you sent me last September."

"I told you it wasn't my fault."

Angela bent again and helped Katherine to her feet. Up close she looked younger than she had a right to, but her breath smelled foul.

"You think you're crazy, right, Katherine?"

Her mother smiled as a flicker of emotion crossed Katherine's face.

"I always knew what you were thinking. But you're not crazy, although you'll probably wish you were." Her voice paused, her expression hesitant. "You see, your father and I are...undead."

The river roared in Katherine's ears. She closed her eyes to wash away the vision before her.

"I've been this way since I died. When I first met your father thirty-five years ago, he was... that way too. When I found out I was pregnant with you I made him swear not to take me until you'd grown up and were on your own."

Katherine opened her eyes to look into her mother's white face. She looked almost as young as when Katherine was a child.

"You look younger," she whispered.

Angela smiled slightly, parting her lips to expose a neat row of sharp looking teeth. "Your father first bit me when I was thirty. Now that I'm an undead, my body is returning to the original state it was in when I was first bitten." Her smile widened. "I'll stay young."

Katherine shook her head. This was too much for her to deal with. She had to be dreaming. She was probably still in the basement, propped up in the kitchen chair beside the garbage bag. When she woke up, she'd have an awful kink in her neck.

The breeze stirred the water beneath the bridge, making it gurgle. Katherine became aware of Daniel standing close beside her. She started. She hadn't heard him move.

"Angela has told me so much about you," he said. A white hand reached up to touch her hair. She shied away.

"I wish I could have seen you grow up but your mother insisted otherwise. She was right of course, but I am glad you've come here to join us."

Katherine's eyes widen. Join them? She took a step back and felt the rail press against her buttocks. The wood beneath her feet creaked.

A shadow passed over her mother's face. "Daniel?"

"Of course, it's natural for you to want to be with your parents. I always believed that was the way it should have been all along." Daniel stepped closer. His face glowed in the darkness, his blue eyes darkening. Behind his pale lips, Katherine saw his tongue lick over two long, pointed incisors.

"Daniel, no!" Angela grabbed his arm and pulled. She managed only to halt him. "This wasn't part of our agreement."

"What's the difference? We can all be together," he said. He looked back at Katherine. "Besides, I haven't fed tonight."

He took another step. With a cry, Angela pounced.

The bridge swayed as they struggled. Holding onto the rail, Katherine backed away. They fought like animals, snarling and snapping. Daniel sank his teeth into Angela's shoulders. Her shriek echoed off the treetops.

Katherine turned and ran. The bridge pitched beneath her feet. Several times she stumbled, falling against the railing, bruising her hip. The snarls of the fight followed her.

Almost to the end of the bridge she stumbled again, landing on her knees. She grabbed for the rail. There was a groan of metal and a piece snapped off in her hand. She landed on her chest, the air pushed out of her, her face over the edge.

The stench of the river filled her nostrils as she gasped for air. Slowly she crawled away from the edge, still clutching the three foot piece of metal railing.

"No!"

Her mother's cry reached her. Katherine looked. Her mother had fallen to her knees, hands scratching uselessly against Daniel's back as he bent over her.

He's killing her, Katherine thought, and then he'll come for me.

She struggled to her feet, trying to recall the vampire lore she knew. Mostly it was from the old Hammer films. Stake through the heart, garlic, sunlight, something about running water. It was all she could remember.

She didn't have a stake, but she did have the railing.

The broken tip was jagged, not exactly a point. Flaking paint scratched her hand as she gripped it, sweat making it slip. The edges dug into her fingers. Her heart pounded in her chest as if she'd run up a flight of stairs too fast. There was only one chance.

Her mother cried out again, weakly. Her hands fluttered slightly. Daniel growled low.

Raising the rail like a javelin, Katherine began to run. The bridge swayed, keeping pace. The darkened forms drew closer, larger. She aimed for the left side of Daniel's back.

He seemed to sense her, straightening. To Katherine he moved in slow motion, his strong back slowly pulling itself erect. She tightened her grip on the rail. Aimed. Thrust.

He shrieked as the rail pierced his back. Droplets of blood splashed back into Katherine's face. She threw all her weight behind the rail, driving it farther. Daniel fell forward, knocking her mother over. Katherine stumbled and landed on his legs. Her left foot slipped over the edge of the walkway. She felt coolness reflected from the water below.

She scrambled off him, clinging to the wooden planks. The bridge swayed, creaking as if to protest all this activity. Katherine reached forward and touched the hem of her mother's dress.

"Momma?"

Angela stirred. She tried to sit up, but her arms trembled violently. "Katherine, help me," she whispered.

Katherine wrapped her arms around her mother and lifted her away, carrying her a few feet. She weighed no more than a bundle of sticks, Katherine thought in dismay.

When released, Angela could not support herself and sank down to the wooden floor. Her skin was no longer white but almost translucent. Her neck and shoulder were torn open, revealing bloodless muscle and scratched bone.

Looking past her, Katherine saw Daniel had not moved. He lay face down, the rail protruding from his back like a mast.

"I'll be right back," she said.

Angela nodded weakly.

Katherine crept forward and turned Daniel over. His face was frozen in an expression of shock, blood staining his mouth like lipstick. The tip of the rail protruded through the front of his shirt almost bashfully.

She returned to her mother and knelt. "He's dead, momma."

Angela raised her hand and tried to touch Katherine's face. "I'm so sorry. I didn't want to hurt you."

Katherine shook her head. "No, I'm the one who's sorry. I shouldn't have found that letter." Her throat dried up, making it difficult to talk. "I wanted to keep everything. I didn't want you to go."

Angela smiled. "I didn't want to leave either. Maybe we were both wrong."

Katherine took her mother's hand, so cold, skin almost clear, and held it to her tear stained cheek.

Neither said anything more. They sat until morning, until the sky began to lighten and the birds began to sing. Angela struggled, trying to pull herself to her feet but she was too weak. Desperately she clutched at Katherine's ankles. The wounds in her neck and shoulder looked blanched, bits of skin flapping in the breeze.

"Help," Angela pleaded. Her voice strained but still didn't get above a whisper.

Katherine knelt down. She wanted to take hold of her mother, comfort her. If she ran quickly she could carry her mother back to the house before the sun was over the horizon. She leaned forward.

"Katherine," her mother whispered.

One of her teeth flashed white in the approaching brightness. Katherine pulled back, startled. She stared at Angela's face. It was her mother's face but the eyes were too dark, too intense, too desperate. Her mother had never looked like that, even in the worst times. Your dignity is all you have, she'd say.

Said.

Mother is dead, Katherine thought. For the first time in three months the thought did not make her want to cry. A calm settled over her. Mother was dead and Katherine had been lucky, so very lucky to have had her. But she was gone now. This creature before her was only a bad copy, a husk.

"I'll stay with you until it's done," Katherine said. She owed her mother, her mother's memory that.

Feeling Angela scrape weakly at her hand, Katherine turned her face to welcome the sun.

Hard Body

Elmer stood in the doorway to the Body Epoch Club and felt slightly nauseous.

His reflection was a sparse nothing in the far wall which was covered with mirrors, his scrawniness made more obvious by the sleek muscled bodies moving to some elaborate choreography. Near the door a row of women pumped away on the life cycles. Tawny thighs moved in rhythm to the driving music. Men, biceps flexing, their large chests barely covered by skimpy muscle shirts, sat on the kayak machines. Their movements blurred, the machines humming. Elmer remembered trying that machine when he toured the club. He could barely manage two rotations.

What am I doing here? he thought. He didn't belong in this atmospheric club with these well toned people. Black metal beams and ducts criss-crossed over his head, fashionable ceiling lights hanging down to illuminate the floor. Colour coordinated machines, black with accents of blue or red or green (depending on the muscle group being worked) gleamed hungrily at him.

He could leave, just pick up his new gym bag, free with the registration fee, the silver logo emblazed on the side, a reflection of the stamp on the machines, and leave. Slink away down the stairs, escape before one of those perfectly sculptured...

"Would you like to sign in?" A smiling woman, blonde hair pulled back in a ponytail. Even her hand looked muscular.

Elmer swallowed.

Okay, here he was, on the life cycles. This wasn't so bad. The seat pinched his narrow buttocks as he began to pedal. Only twenty minutes. He could handle that. No more Mr. Weakling, no more inhalers.

After two minutes he was panting. The cycle seemed to have a life of its own, easing up, then getting so hard he almost had to stand to push the pedals down. God, this was killing him! What was he doing here?

The image of Douglas Kerr, new head accountant, floated into his mind. Douglas was never embarrassed to wear short sleeves. In fact, his arms bulged beneath his sleeves, like a beast ready to rip through the fabric. Everyone noticed Douglas, enough for him to get the promotion that should have been Elmer's.

Elmer pedalled harder.

Just under two hours later, Elmer was finished. On the subway home, he almost fell asleep, the gentle back and forth motion of the train making him drowsy. He managed to get off at his stop and shuffle home. Every inch of his body was tired, from his scalp to his toes. Was it possible, he wondered, for your eyebrows to be tired?

The next day at work the stiffness was so bad he could barely lift a pencil.

Over the next two months he increased his work outs to three times a week. The difference wasn't quite what he'd expected. No huge bulging muscles appeared on his arms, no massive thighs erupted on his legs. His chest didn't expand to rip through his shirt. Instead his arms and legs hardened like lead. No longer did his flesh hang off him like a bad suit. He felt more energetic, more alive than before. He rarely needed his inhaler any more, even though he still carried it. Short sleeves weren't so embarrassing but although his arms looked lean, they weren't the impressive rippling of solid, bulky muscles. He was whipcord lean but that wasn't what he wanted. He wanted beefcake.

By the end of February, work was beginning to pile up. Tax season meant a lot of overtime. Elmer stayed later and later in the office. Six o'clock leavings soon became eight o'clock, became nine. He was lucky if he made it to the club by ten, but he continued to go. Tax season, while the most exciting time, was also the most stressful. Elmer was surprised to find that exercising helped dissolve the stress. A particularly convoluted problem melted away under the onslaught of free weights. Pressure from his manager faded with leg curls.

Working out later also meant less lineups at the equipment. After nine, few people worked out their bodies at the gleaming machines of chrome and steel. But those who did were different. The women were elegant, all rippling thighs and arms, iron hard stomachs peeking through their workout uniforms. Elmer found it hard not to stare as they walked by, rounded buttocks moving smoothly, parted by the thong of their suits. The men were almost as gorgeous. Massive biceps and pectorals barely covered by muscle shirts made Elmer feel very small and inadequate. He wondered briefly about steroids but the men weren't grotesque in their fitness. Veins didn't bulge from their muscles and they could bring their arms down to their sides. They moved with a sleekness Elmer couldn't help but admire.

Where did they get such sleekness, Elmer wondered and with a pang of disappointment he realized he would never be like that. This was the best he would get, and although it was better than the sickly, weak child he had been, he was beginning to see that it wasn't enough.

Elmer turned to the man on the life cycle next to him.

"How long have you been here?" he asked.

"Three years," the man said. As introduction, he continued: "I'm Gil. This is a good club. Clean like this all the time." He bobbed his head in time to the pumping of his legs.

Elmer studied the other man's form. Healthy but not like the others, not so heavily muscled.

"Three years," Elmer repeated. "Been good for you?"

"You kidding? I was a mess before I joined. Couldn't walk up a flight of stairs without passing out, smoked like a chimney. I quit smoking two years ago. Don't even miss it. Never felt better."

Elmer nodded. "What about them?" He gestured toward the corner where two men lifted large weights. As he watched, the tallest one, dark hair pulled back from his face in an unruly ponytail, finished. The man settled the weight down and walked over to a bar, mechanically adjustable for height. Strapping into gravity boots attached to the bar, he raised the bar until his head didn't touch the floor. Slowly, then with increasing strength, he began to do situps.

Beside him, Gil leaned closer. "He's a lifer." His whisper was conspiratorial.

"A lifer?"

"Yeah, there's three membership levels."

Elmer frowned. "They only told me about two."

"They don't mention the third one until you've been here at least a year, but you can't qualify until you've been here for five. Basic membership is just for the club. You got that. Next level gets you access to the extras, certified physiotherapist, masseuse, chiropractor. Very exclusive. Third membership level is the lifers. For twenty-five percent of your annual income for the rest of your life, they guarantee you'll look like that." Gil hooked a thumb over at the man doing the upside down situps.

Elmer's eyes widened in surprise. "Guarantee it? How can they do that?"

Gil shrugged. "Don't know. I don't know any of the lifers."

"Steroids?" Elmer whispered.

"Don't think so. At least I've never heard anything like that." Gil nodded at the man on the bar. "They says he's the owner and..."

"And?" Elmer prompted.

"They say he's almost sixty-five."

Elmer had suspected his leg was being pulled and now he knew it. "No way."

"I'm serious," Gil said. "Sixty-five. He developed the lifer technique."

"Why haven't you signed up then?" Elmer asked.

"Don't have the minimum."

"What minimum? I thought you said twenty-five percent of your income."

"It is, but there's a minimum of fifty thousand dollars. I don't make that."

Gil's life cycle beeped then, signalling his session over. He climbed off the bike. "See ya." He moved over to the arm pulls.

Elmer continued pedalling. He still had another fifteen minutes left. For that entire time, he stared at the man doing situps on the bar. Finally when the life cycle beeped, he climbed off.

The man on the bar was still doing situps. It didn't even look like he'd broken a sweat.

At the office the next day, Elmer actually found five minutes in which to breathe. Fifty thousand, he thought, tapping his pencil on the edge of his keyboard. A hell of a lot of money for an exercise club. Besides, how the hell could somebody guarantee that anybody would look like that? Didn't genetics have anything to do with it? Wasn't that why there were all these creams and pills and plastic thigh exercisers that promised to work and always failed? If there was actually some way to guarantee that anybody could look like that, somebody would have found it before now and mass marketed it. The secret wouldn't be tucked away in one exercise club.

Stupid, Elmer thought, just stupid.

His phone ran, and the day continued.

Pressure at work increased. Elmer now brown bagged lunch and dinner, eating both at his desk, surrounded by printouts, two computers displaying different printouts and a perpetually ringing phone. If they didn't have to let him leave at night to sleep, Elmer knew his bosses would have found a way. But he didn't feel as stressed as previous years, not nearly so close to the end of his rope. He increased his workouts to four times a week.

One night, it was almost midnight by the time he was able to get to the club. The main room was empty as he used his pass card to get in. Diligently he signed in and slipped into the change room. First the life cycle. He headed for the gleaming row just in front of the mirrors.

The song playing over the speakers faded. Silence, filled with expectation, filled the void then another song began. Heavy bonging bass reverberated through the room, in Elmer's chest. A Russian composer, he knew, but couldn't recall the name.

The staff office door opened and the dark haired man stepped out. Elmer remembered him doing the upside down situps. As he strolled toward the free weights, his movements were elegant, cat-like, with a gracefulness Elmer found hard to associate with such a physique. Lifting one of the barbells onto a stand, he added five plates to each end. Elmer couldn't imagine how much that weighted. He couldn't imagine lifting it.

The man pulled his dark hair back and tied it in a ponytail. Then he lifted the bar and began doing arm curls.

They were alone in the club. Elmer realized he hadn't seen Gil in a while. The last time had been two weeks ago and the man had come in to ride the life cycle for only twenty minutes. Elmer was certain that Gil had lost muscle tone. The trimness in his body was gone, replaced with a suggestion of softness. Elmer was surprised and then disgusted. How could Gil let that happen? He never would. He was going to get better, get stronger, get those muscles.

While Elmer completed his workout, the owner, as Elmer thought of him, only did three exercises, all for his arms. By the time Elmer finished, he was drenched in sweat, his heart pounding vigorously. He wrapped a towel around his neck, breathing hard, and looked over at the owner. The man didn't have a drop of perspiration on him. He caught Elmer's glance in the mirror and nodded. Then a slow, leisurely smile spread over his generous lips.

The next day, Elmer took a whole half hour to figure out what it would take to get a lifetime membership.

"I'm sorry, sir, we don't offer lifetime member-ships to members who have been with the club for less than five years. It's policy, sir."

Elmer snorted impatiently. "Policies can be changed. Why do I have to wait?"

"I'm just telling you what I've been told, sir. All members must be with the club for a minimum of five year before they are eligible for lifetime membership."

"Who can I talk to about applying early?"

"Well, you could try speaking to the owner, Mr. Trenton, but I don't think he's ever changed the policy."

"How do I speak to Mr. Trenton?"

The office was more spacious than he'd imagined. But then if some of your club members were paying in excess of $15,000 a year for life, you could probably afford a large office, Elmer thought. All the chairs were leather, including the one Elmer sat in. He rubbed one hand over the smooth black surface. It felt cool against his fingertips. The window afforded a spectac-ular view of the city, facing toward the lake. He watched a column of smoke from a smoke stack drift lazily across the tops of the buildings. The fading sun cast long shadows between the towers, the darkness like a rising sea. Soon it would rise high enough to engulf the buildings, plunging them into night.

An electronic shade lowered from the ceiling with a loud hum. Startled Elmer blinked rapidly, hands pressing against the cool leather. Slowly the city disappeared behind the shade and he was left in the artificial light cast from the ceiling.

Behind him the office door opened. Elmer fought the urge to turn around. Footsteps approached on his right, quickly passing. He looked up. The owner, Mr. Trenton, came around the desk and sat down. As he leaned back, he crossed his hands on his lap, a stillness settling over him. Dark hair framed his face as generous lips smiled slightly.

"Mr. Johnson, I understand you have a request?"

"I would like more information about your lifetime membership."

Trenton nodded slowly. The dark curls bobbed. "I see. I'm sorry but lifetime membership is not available to members who have been with us for less than five year."

Elmer pursed his lips. "Why?"

"Being a lifetime member takes a lot of commitment as well as money. We have very few of them and I reserve the right to determine how high the level of commitment is from each member. The greater majority is satisfied with the basic membership or the deluxe membership."

"You guarantee a high level of fitness with your lifetime memberships?"

"Mr. Johnson, I guarantee only that if my plans are followed, a high level of fitness will result. If you don't follow my plans, I can't be responsible."

"What kind of plan do the lifetime members get?" Elmer asked.

"I'm sorry, Mr. Johnson, I've said enough about that. If you feel your program is not challenging enough at present, we can certainly do a reevaluation." His gaze swept up and down Elmer's body as though he could see through Elmer's clothes, through the skin itself to his muscles, his organs, the very fibre of his being.

"I don't want a reevaluation," Elmer said.

Trenton smiled again and shrugged. "I'm sorry, Mr. Johnson, that's all I can do."

Elmer skipped the club that night and went home. He sat on the orange and brown fabric couch in his living room, rubbing the armrest. It was scratchy and worn, not at all like the cool elegance of Trenton's office.

Who am I kidding, Elmer thought. There was no way they would let him be a lifetime member. Even if they would allow him, where would he get fifty thousand dollars a year? What could they possibly do that would be worth that kind of money anyway, even if he had it? Forget it, he told himself. He still looked pretty good. He flexed his arm, feeling the muscle tighten, the tendons work. His skin had a healthy glow, but still his arm was, well, skinny.

Working too much, he thought. Once this tax season was over he would take a vacation.

After the madness of April, he was able to settle down to normal hours, able to get the club before eight. But he didn't like it, it had a different feel. More people milled about, using the machines, talking, rustling about. He found it unsettling. He watched them from his life cycle, pumping along. They seemed to do more talking than working out. What was this, some kind of social club? He was now as much of a hard body as they were, and they were nothing special. Every time the door swung open, he found himself glancing up, expecting one of the lifetime members to stroll in. A hush would fall over the room, even the pounding, driving bass music would seem more subdued. All eyes would watch as the lifer walked to the bar with the gravity boots and began those upside down situps.

In his vision, this lifer had Elmer's face.

Elmer began going to the club later and later.

He had to become a lifer, he knew that now. The club at midnight was where he belonged. He liked walking down the street toward the club, looking up to see its lit windows beckoning him on. Once inside, he forgot about the city. It ceased to exist for him, he was encased by a bubble of light and glistening machines which protected him from the ever encroaching darkness.

The lifers, all glistening muscles and rippling stomachs exposed through the veil of workout shorts and muscle shirts, ignored him at first. He was not one of them. But eventually, as he continued to encroach on their domain late at night, they glanced at him, dark eyes curious, the muscles of their necks and back stirring as they looked over. Soon they would give him a nod, acknowledging his presence.

It was satisfying but not enough. He wanted to be one of them, but how could he ever afford that kind of money? Accountants just didn't make that much. There had to be a way, he thought, as he picked at his dinner salad.

The next day he began to research the Body Epoch Club.

Everything seemed normal. Incorporation, leasing of the building, tax returns. He could access it all through freedom of information, or he could pull a few strings and see what wasn't so easily accessible. Like the fact that the building the club leased was actually owned by a Mr. Theodore Trenton. Possibly the club owner? But the building was fifty years old and had only had one owner. His father perhaps? But Elmer remembered the rumours. Sixty-five. Impossible, the man couldn't be over forty.

The club was fifteen years old, quite an accomplishment for an exercise club. But none of the tax returns showed anything about lifetime memberships. Could it be included in the assets? He spent three nights recalculating. Finally at three in the morning, he threw down his pencil.

He couldn't believe it, they weren't reporting the lifetime memberships! His heart began to pound.

It wasn't even very well hidden. If someone had even an inclination they would find the discrepancy between the income of the club and the amount they expended in salaries, equipment and profit-sharing to the owner. He didn't know how many lifers there were, he'd seen at least seven and he wasn't there every night. Seven times a minimum of fifty thousand meant three hundred and fifty thousand a year disappeared under the table, tax free!

Elmer made a note to make an appointment with Mr. Trenton and then didn't sleep a wink.

At seven o'clock the next evening he was once again sitting in that leather chair, clutching his worn briefcase on his lap. He rechecked his figures one last time, ignoring the panoramic view of the city. With a click and a hum, the window blind drew down, blocking out the view. Again Trenton entered once the blinds were down and this time Elmer turned around.

Trenton wore a dark suit, his elegant body draped exquisitely by the fabric. As he walked to the desk, the clothing tightened and released around the muscles of his thighs and arms. Massive hands rested on the desk as he turned his dark eyes toward Elmer. He smiled.

"Mr. Johnson, a pleasure to see you again."

"Yes, it is a pleasure," Elmer said. "And I hope it continues to be, if we come to a mutually acceptable agreement."

Trenton's perfectly shaped eyebrows lifted.

"I've been looking at your income tax returns," Elmer said. "I'm an accountant, you see."

The smile on Trenton's face slowly faded. "I believe those records are confidential."

"Are they? I think the revenue service would be interested in taking a closer look at them, once they've heard of the discrepancies I discovered."

"Discrepancies?"

Elmer opened his briefcase and withdrew several sheets of paper. "I've been looking over your expenditures. They just don't match up with the records you've been giving to the revenue service. I couldn't find anything to match the income of your lifetime memberships." Elmer shook his head. "Very strange."

Trenton's eyes narrowed until they were tiny black orbs in the expanse of his handsome face. A few crow's feet wrinkles formed around the edges of his eyes, a few frown lines appeared but he still didn't look sixty-five.

"How much do you want?" he growled.

"No, Mr. Trenton, you misunderstand. I believe we can come to a mutually acceptable agreement."

Massive hands rested lightly on the desk blotter. Elmer noticed how finely manicured the fingernails were.

"Continue."

"As I have said, I want to become a lifetime member," Elmer said. He held up a hand to stop Trenton's interruption. "I understand your policy, however, you have a problem that I can help you with. The assets from the lifetime memberships are not hidden very well, eventually the revenue service will discover the discrepancy with or without my calling it to their attention. I can solve that before it happens and continue to make sure it doesn't happen. If you make me a lifetime member."

Trenton stared at him, his expression unreadable, the muscles of his jaw flexing. Elmer held his briefcase in his lap, trying not to grip the papers so tightly. He didn't want Trenton to know how badly he wanted this. If Trenton called his bluff, refused the membership, Elmer would have to go to the revenue service. Not only would the club be shut down, questions would also be asked as to how Elmer came across such information. It could be awkward and potentially damaging to any contacts he had. And he would never become a lifetime member, never reach his goal.

"No one has ever become a lifetime member before they've completed five years with the club," Trenton said. His voice was a low growl. "It isn't just an arbitrary rule. I need the time to study the member, be certain of his appropriateness." His eyes refocused on Elmer, boring into his soul.

Elmer hunched his shoulders. He'd pushed too far. He knew it.

"Perhaps you are appropriate," Trenton said. "Come back at midnight. We'll find out then." He reached for the phone, using the gesture to dismiss Elmer.

Outside on the sidewalk, watching the last of the sun's rays bleed across the sky, Elmer was confused. He'd been sure Trenton was about to refuse him, throw him out of the office, whatever. Instead he was supposed to return at midnight. Maybe that's when Trenton would deal with him. Images of gangster movies he'd seen drifted through his mind. But this wasn't the mafia it was an exercise club. One hundred and five thousand dollars a year is a lot of money, maybe worth killing for.

But Trenton said he might be appropriate for a lifetime membership.

Could Elmer pass up the promise of his dream fulfilled?

He went hunting for a coffee shop.

The sign on the door said the club was closed

for a special function. Elmer hesitated then tried the door knob. It turned and opened, the room beyond beckoning him forward.

The music had been turned off, leaving a stillness behind that Elmer found unnerving. After all the movement and motion of his other visits, this hush held all the weight of a pregnant pause.

"Mr. Johnson, please come in."

The woman motioning him forward was tall and elegant, sculptured muscles gleaming with health. Her lush red lips smiled invitingly. He'd seen her a couple of times, late at night in the club. A lifer.

He followed her into a large room, lit only by candles circling the walls. Nine men and women waited and Elmer recognized several of them. They, like the woman who'd brought him in, were lifers. He swallowed.

Trenton entered from another door. He'd changed into a muscle shirt and biking shorts which accentuated the musculature of his thighs. He stepped into the centre of the circle of waiting lifetime members and turned to face Elmer.

"Everyone is aware of the situation. As this

is delicate and concerns us all, I have asked you here to consider the matter. Any thoughts?"

"I've seen Mr. Johnson several times in the club. He appears to be conscientious," one of the men spoke up.

"He's only been a member for a few months," one of the women protested. "How do we know he has the commitment to become one of us?"

"I think his actions show quite a bit of determination," said the woman who'd brought him in. She flashed another smile of her red lips. "I think he would have the commitment."

They argued back and forth for several minutes, Trenton standing like a silent sentry in the centre of them. He stared at Elmer and Elmer stared back. This was part of the test, he realized. He would remain calm, despite his pounding heart. His hands felt sticky but he refused to wipe them.

Finally the conversation exhausted itself and all the lifers stood looking expectantly at Trenton. Trenton stirred, as if waking from a deep sleep.

"I initiated the five year membership requirement as a guide to enable me to judge the appropriateness of each candidate for lifetime membership," he said. Although his voice was barely above a whisper, it carried throughout the room. "It has been sufficient for most of you but I believe Mr. Johnson has proven to be an exception."

Elmer held his breath, his heart thudding in his chest.

"Your conditions for lifetime membership are as follows, Mr. Johnson: your services regarding our little tax problem for the life of your membership as well as twenty-five percent of your income at a minimum of twenty thousand dollars per year." Trenton paused. "Are these conditions acceptable?"

Elmer felt dizzy until he realized he'd forgotten to breathe. He gulped in air.

"I accept," he gasped.

Trenton smiled. "Now we will tell you exactly what lifetime membership entails. You are allowed all the privileges of the deluxe members. One small act will guarantee that you will become as fit as you desire for the rest of your life." His lips curled upward. "Step forward, Mr. Johnson."

Elmer stepped forward into the centre toward Trenton. Although no one touched him, he felt compelled by their stares as if their wills contained invisible hands, forcing him forward to stand a foot from Trenton.

"This final act you may not speak about to anyone other than your fellow lifetime members. To do so means expulsion." His eyes darkened, betraying a fearsome fury. Elmer pressed his hands together to stop them from trembling.

Trenton's large hand grabbed Elmer's shoulder and squeezed. Elmer felt his muscles slide against bone and winced. Trenton pulled him even closer.

"Welcome to the club, Elmer," Trenton hissed and bared his fangs.

Elmer gasped and tried to pull away, but Trenton's grip was too strong. The scent of Trenton's shampoo invaded Elmer's nostrils then a sharp pain engulfed him, sending him spinning off into a haze of red, punctuated with flashes of scarlet pain.

He opened his eyes to find himself kneeling on the floor. He stared at the black rubber tiles, trying to orient himself. He felt as jagged as the tiles' puzzle-like edges. What had happened? Then he remembered. Trenton. Teeth. Pain. Elmer looked at his shirt. It was stained with blood.

Two of the lifers helped him to his feet, supporting him. Trenton stood in front of him, blotting his mouth with a white handkerchief.

"Almost done, Elmer, and then you'll be one of us, for a lifetime." He grinned and Elmer noticed the canines, just a shade sharper than the other teeth, not overly large, not gaudy like movie vampires.

"There are two steps, the first I drink from you, the second step is you drink from the sacrifice. Afterward you will be a lifetime member, Elmer, just like you wanted." He motioned to the far end of the room. Two of the men broke away from the circle and retreated to the door. After a moment they returned, dragging the limp form of a man between them. They dumped him unceremoniously on the floor in front of Trenton.

One of Trenton's aerobic shoes nudged the man. He stirred.

"This man has neglected his workouts," Trenton said. "Not only that, he has encouraged others to do so as well. We do not tolerate such sloppiness or such blatant undermining of our rules. Accordingly, I have exercised my option and cancelled his membership."

The man looked up. Gil.

Elmer stared at him, stared at the arms, once trim like his now a little flabby, his legs also losing muscle tone. Gil opened his mouth lazily, looking like a doped fish.

"Deal with him, Elmer, complete your membership requirements and become a lifetime member."

The two men beside him released him and Elmer stumbled forward. He felt weak, drained like a sieve. If he became a lifetime member he would never feel this way again, never feel fatigue, or weariness, or death. He would become perfect, like all these other people. He looked at them, firm muscles, sleek skin. The women were young, smooth faces even when they smiled. The men practically reeked of vitality. Complete the membership requirements.

Gil stared up at him, faded blue eyes watery and indistinct. Gil a regular club member, who strove to keep himself fit but had slipped away. Human nature. Arms getting flabby, legs and stomach drooping. White hairs sprinkled through his thinning brown hair. He smelled of sweat.

Lifetime membership, thought Elmer. Seven thousand dollars. Twenty-five percent of annual income.

He could handle that.

Elmer licked his sharpened canines and jumped into his latest workout.

Back In The Day

As he passed the first row of tombstones the lights flashed on, spraying colours and scents across the graveyard in a kaleidoscope display that shimmered in the night air. Already he could make out the figures that jumped out from behind the tombstones and crypts. They raised goblets toward him as music blared out.

"Happy Death Day!"

Vincent Molliare maintained a neutral expression as people came up to congratulate him, shake his hand or slap him on the back. It was all he could do to stop himself from slapping them right back.

As the party got underway, Vincent retreated to the bar, set up outside a large mausoleum. He gulped down one glass of blood before taking another and sitting at one end to nurse it. He leaned his elbows on the bar, manners be damned, and reached for the bowl of peanuts. The peanuts didn't fill him up, no food did anymore, but he still liked the crunch of them. Since late 1938, he'd been on a "liquid diet" as he liked to call it. Besides, being busy with peanuts helped him hide.

He'd quite enjoyed being a vampire back at the beginning. With the popularity of Bela Lugosi as Dracula, Vincent got to dress formally and wear a cape. It suited his tall, thin frame. With enough Brill cream, he could smooth down the black curls on his head and comb them sleek. Women swooned. Men trembled. Now that had been the time to be a vampire.

Not like today. The twenty-fourth century was unkind to vampires.

Fog machines spewed fog forth as people danced around the tombstones. The flashing of their glowing clothing gave Vincent a headache. He stared at the bowl of peanuts. How long before he could slip away?

A short, red-haired girl landed on the seat beside him.

"Hey Uncle Vinnie," she said.

"I'm not your uncle," he said by rote. "I assume this was your idea, Celine?"

She smiled, exposing long, sharp white teeth. "I figured you need some cheering up for today."

"I am not depressed."

She shrugged. Her long sleeved top rippled colour across her body. The stockings on her legs, echoed behind. Vincent frowned. She noticed and laughed.

"You should have more dignity," he said.

"I do have dignity," she said. "It's just different than yours. You like the old fashioned look of capes…"

"It's not old fashioned."

"…and I like the newer looks. We're different, Uncle Vinnie."

"Stop calling me that," he murmured. "Vampires aren't uncles."

She slung her arm around his shoulders. "But your sire sired my sire. That makes us related." She signaled the bartender. "Come on, I'll get you a glass of blood."

"I've got one, thanks." He tapped the half full wine glass.

"Well, drink up. We're celebrating."

"No, we are not."

Celine removed her arm from his shoulders. "Do you really want to sit here and mope?"

He took a large swallow from his glass, draining it. He used the napkin to blot his mouth. "No, I'm leaving."

She hopped off the bar stool. "But the party just started."

"And for me it's ended." He skirted around the dancers and headed for the entrance to the cemetery then stopped as he noticed her tagging along.

"Go away, Celine."

She folded her arms across her chest. The effect sent a stream of colour up her arms and down her torso. Her mouth parted and he saw the tip of her fangs. She'd dared to unsheathe at him?

"Don't bare your fangs at me, young lady!"

She looked startled and her hand went up to her mouth. "Oh, I didn't mean... Uncle Vinnie!"

But he had already slipped through the cemetery gate and into the night. Not that it mattered much anymore. The protective atmospheric fields filtered out all harmful effects of the sun and it was so effective that vampires could now walk in the day. Disgusting, he thought. Creatures of the night walking in the daytime. Most didn't even drink blood, just ingested capsules and water that supplied all the nutrients needed for a healthy vampire.

Vincent hated it.

With the capsules and the daytime walking, vampires weren't feared anymore, never mind hunted. They wore over ear/over eye connectors just like everyone else, jacking into the computers and socializing with humans. Socializing! How could any self-respecting vampire do such a thing? They were supposed to be loners, scavenging on the edge of human society. Now they were regular citizens, holding jobs, shopping, doing everything the humans did. How many of them at even been at his party?

Maybe he was really just too old for this modern world. Maybe he was too old fashioned. With all the neon and glowing hoverlights, there were barely any decent shadows to lurk in and even when he did find some, no one was horrified or even startled when he leapt out.

As he walked, his cloak swirled around his feet. Maybe it was time to give it up. But he didn't think he could embrace this new culture. It just wasn't in him. He'd been a vampire too long, too trapped in the old way of thinking. Sure it was easy for Celine, she was only a hundred and twelve. Try tripling that, my dear, he thought. He'd never really liked change. Adapting to being a vampire was the last change he'd managed.

Unfortunately, change ignored his desires and went right on overtaking the world.

He turned off the main street and headed down a side street. The hoverlights were more spaced out, allowing for pockets of darkness. He could almost pretend to be stalking someone at night.

As he walked, listening to his own echoing footsteps, he noticed other footfalls behind him. Someone was following him. Probably Celine, still trying to find a way to cheer him up and coax him back to the party. He appreciated her efforts but he didn't want cheering up tonight of all nights. This night was his, to spend anyway he wished, the anniversary of his last night as human and first night as vampire. He didn't want to hurt her feelings, she was really a dear friend, but enough was enough.

"Celine..." He turned to confront her. The walkway was empty. The nearest hoverlight was almost ten feet away. Darkness encroached, masking the details of the surrounding buildings, turning vegetation into hulking shadows. Not Celine? Then who was following him?

Vincent shrugged and continued on his way. Probably someone who didn't want to be bothered, just like himself. He had no intention of forcing his company on anyone tonight. Let everyone have their own private walks.

The footsteps started up again, still behind him and going his way, maintaining their distance. Vincent tried not to let it bother him. He'd had more than his share of wannabees. It always happened after every revival of the old 2D vampire movies. But he never said yes and he certainly wasn't going to now. Better to keep ignoring whoever it was and they'd get bored soon enough.

He heard the creak of wood and the telltale hum of a wire being pulled back. The sound reminded him of something. He could almost remember... He felt the air shift as something let go.

With vampire speed, he jumped aside. The arrow soared past where he'd been and slammed into a tree trunk several yards ahead. Vincent blinked and walked over to it. Wood, about right where his heart would be if he'd stayed in the same spot. He turned around.

A figure stood wearing a billowing brown coat and a wide brimmed hat pulled over its face. Thick leather gloves held a crossbow. As Vincent watched, the figure loaded another arrow into the bow.

"I will kill you, creature of the undead," the figure called. "You will know my vengeance."

"Are you kidding me?" Vincent said.

The figure raised the crossbow.

Guess not, Vincent thought. As the arrow released, Vincent jumped aside again. This time he felt the air ripple by his shoulder as the arrow flew by. The figure had anticipated Vincent's jump and changed the aim. Vincent felt his whole body tingling with something he'd thought he'd forgotten.

Excitement.

The figure pulled out another arrow. He'd had enough chances, Vincent thought. No more freebies.

"Try to seek vengeance," Vincent called. "Be careful it isn't death you find instead!"

He spun away, making sure to grab the corner of his cape so it would billow out behind him. He ran off, heading deeper into the neighbourhood, angling toward the park. They had even fewer hoverlights positioned there.

He allowed himself to actually move at vampire speed, something he hardly ever needed to do anymore. The landscape blurred around him. Within a few minutes, he reached the edge of the park, some three miles from where he'd been walking. He didn't even feel winded. It felt good to run wild like that.

And he'd given a pretty good exit line, he thought. Dramatic without being too flowery, with just the right amount of threat. He was quite pleased with it.

As he stepped into the park, he started to wonder who would seek vengeance on him. It wasn't like he'd killed anyone for two hundred years. There wasn't the need and with vampires being regular citizens, he didn't really want to face the jail sentence. Life without parole took on a whole new meaning for the undead. Besides, even before that he hadn't exactly been the real killer type. He'd preferred to take just enough. It left fewer questions. He'd always been more interested in frightening than actually killing. So who would be seeking revenge on him?

Maybe it was a misunderstanding. Maybe the figure had mistaken him for someone else. But he'd never heard of any other vampire who walked around in a cape. Maybe the figure was after a human, but that didn't fit either. He'd anticipated

Vincent's movement as a vampire. So what was really going on?

He had no time to figure it out. Better get moving, he always thought better when he was moving. He stepped off the path and into the park. The scent of cut grass and earth came to him on the breeze. The rustle of leaves and branches led him deeper inside. He was particularly fond of this park; it started off civilized with the even lawn and manicured bushes, then as it progressed, it turned into forest. Wild maple and oak extended a thick canopy and even though there was a marked path with fencing, he could easily jump it and disappear into the underbrush. He just had to move fast enough to avoid any hovercams; he didn't want to pay the fine.

Although he didn't anticipate the figure catching up with him any time soon, he raced toward the forest. He never underestimated an opponent; that was how he'd survived so long. If the figure did track him to the forest, it would have a hard time finding him there. Then Vincent could circle back and…

And what?

Technically, he should be contacting the authorities and reporting the attack but what kind of vampire would he be if he let someone else fight his battles? He might as well let the figure stake him. No, he would have to deal with this person on his own. Certainly the unprovoked attack gave him grounds to defend himself. If he ever had to justify his actions, he knew he could do it and be persuasive at it. Another bonus of being a vampire.

The looming shape of the forest darkened the horizon. His ears caught the flurry of night insects and the coo of owls. He concentrated and shifted his weight. Now his footsteps were a brief whistle on the ground, leaving the smallest scuff in his wake. He flowed past the tree trunks with the merest flitter of his cape. It had been so long since he'd had to use these skills. It invigorated him. How he'd missed this!

He heard the crunch of footsteps entering the forest. It couldn't possibly be his follower but who else would be here at this time of night? How had the figure anticipated Vincent coming to the park? Maybe it really did know about the vampire. If it did, it would know that Vincent preferred the outdoors and never slunk around buildings. Damn, Vincent thought, I should not have come to the park. But how could he have known how prepared his follower would be?

Time to go on the offensive. He was a vampire, he was supposed to be the hunter not the prey. Time to act like it.

Vincent moved deeper into the forest, off the path and into the denser underbrush. He slipped through bushes like the wind, mimicking its brush against the leaves. He left no footprints, no trace. Still he listened hard and heard the whisper of the footsteps following behind.

This follower was an excellent tracker, someone with experience with vampires, he thought. A true vampire hunter. He hadn't seen one of those for years. The idea sent a shiver of excitement through him. A worthy foe.

An idea formed in Vincent's mind. He smiled to himself as he turned north. Just a short distance away, he knew of a gully leading to a small waterfall. Under the stars it was a beautiful sight and perfect for an ambush. Just as long as his follower kept following...

Vincent picked up speed. Soon the faint brush of his follower's footsteps faded but Vincent didn't worry. If this vampire hunter was as good as suspected, he would be able to track. The faintest mark on the ground or the slight bend of a leaf would lead him on the way. Vincent couldn't make it too easy. Or too obvious.

The trickle of water came to his ears and soon distinguished itself as the waterfall. A deeper darkness grew ahead. He sensed the dip in the ground as it sloped downward. He followed, sidestepping the occasional root or rock. He now had his full night vision and even in the faint moonlight, everything glowed. Vegetation held a dark green sheen. The ground looked heavy grey. The rushing water moved inky black. Vincent stepped lightly, his feet skimming the ground, avoiding the wet mud. The rush of the water-fall filled his ears, his senses. He slipped around behind it to nestle in the slight depression behind the water. Two inches from his nose, the wall of water rushed down. The sound of it filled his mind and his being then he cancelled it away, allowing his senses to reach beyond the water.

The roar dulled in his ears and he focused on the chirp of the insects and the rustle of the leaves. After a few moments, he heard a subtle shift on the ground. Footsteps. His follower was indeed as good a tracker as Vincent had suspected.

Good.

Vincent waited. He became a part of the rock behind him. His breath became the breeze. The shifts became shuffles as the follower came closer. Vincent no longer waited, he just was a part of the grove.

Through the black curtain of water, a dark image slipped across the green vegetation. Vincent blinked once to focus his vision. He could almost make out the brown coat. The hat still covered the face. One hand clutched the crossbow, the other held a wooden stake. The sight of it almost caused Vincent's heart to thud but he controlled it. Soon, the figure would be close enough soon and then that stake would no longer be any threat at all.

Or would it? This hunter was better than any Vincent had ever seen before. Obviously he had done his research. Would he have anticipated

Vincent's hiding place? If he knew Vincent liked forests he might know some details of how Vincent attacked.

Stop, Vincent thought, but the fear was already slithering across his body. He held himself still like a part of the rock. His concentration began fragmenting. Already the sound of the rushing water leaked into his awareness. Visual stimulus eroded his focus. He wouldn't be able to hold on for much longer. Damn, he usually liked his victim to be closer, within arms reach. Easier to overpower them that way.

That was it. The hunter knew Vincent's habits. Maybe Vincent should do something completely out of the ordinary. Maybe that would give him the upper hand.

Fear and excitement twisted his stomach. He would have to time it precisely. He focused on his senses again, tuning them to the hunter. The hum of the water faded. The flood of stimulation from the surrounding landscape dimmed. Now he could make out the texture of the brown coat, how it hung open, the belt tucked into the side pocket. The leather gloves creaked as the figure tightened his grip on the crossbow, passing it across the wall of water. He clutched the stake in his left hand. Vincent watched, breathing deeply, slowing the image down in his brain, speeding up his own perceptions, readying his own reactions.

As the hunter twisted to the left, sweeping with the crossbow, the left hand was out of sight. He exposed his right side…

Vincent exploded out through the water. The hunter started a slow turn back. Vincent slammed into him and they sprawled on the ground. The hunter slid in the mud. He hung on to the crossbow but it was trapped between them. Vincent leaned heavy on his right and trapped the hunter's left arm. The hunter's hand flailed, still clutching the wooden stake. Vincent roared. His fangs unsheathed. The hunter twisted beneath him, fighting to release his left arm. Vincent grabbed his shoulder and head, pressing both apart, exposing the soft neck. The crossbow, trapped between them, pinched his ribs but Vincent didn't care. Blood lust flowed over him. This was who he was; this was what it was to be a vampire.

He lunged down, fangs piercing the flesh of the hunter's neck. Blood filled Vincent's mouth, warm, tangy, so much sweeter than even the high grade blood served at the bars. He swallowed and then swallowed again until…

The taste was wrong. Metallic, bitter. He wrenched his mouth away, spitting, wiping his hand across his lips. Not human, no way was this blood human. Vincent sat up. The hunter lay still, as if switched off.

Switched off…

Vincent grabbed the shirt and ripped it open. Exposure to the air started the chain reaction of particles that coalesced into infra red words scrolling across its chest.

"Hugh's Man Specialized Androids – the Android for All Occasions. Fully designed and programmed to your specifications. Reusable or recyclable. Serial number REUSE7534AZ779 personal message follows: Happy Death Day, Uncle Vinnie! I know you'll win! My undying love, Celine."

The infra red message glowed for a minute longer then faded, leaving Vincent sitting in the mud beside the inanimate android. The expense and trouble Celine had gone to give him such an elaborate gift, the experience of being hunted and hunting again. He had not felt so alive in years. Yes, this game…

Could go on again, if he wanted, he realized. He didn't have to pine for the old ways, he could experience them any time he liked. In this world of vampires living like humans he could choose what he wanted. He had options. He could do both.

It took him some time before he found the reset button on the android's belt. It responded to his command to stand and wait. Getting up out of the mud, Vincent still felt a tug of unease at how the android held the crossbow and stake. But both hands were loose, relaxed. No threat now, until Vincent wanted it. Until Vincent wanted to play again.

And he could decide exactly how he wanted to play. He could re-experience an old hunt or try something new. Maybe this modern world had things to offer after all.

"Come on," Vincent said to the android. It trudged after him as he returned through the park. Mud soaked into Vincent's pants and clung to his cape, dragging it down. It weighed heavy on his shoulders, heavier with each step. He'd been holding onto it for so long, for several hundred years. Maybe it was time to let it go. Maybe it was time to stop pining for a past that had never really existed.

Vincent shrugged his shoulders. The cape slipped off and fell to the ground in a splat. The android stopped then stepped around it. For a moment, Vincent thought about picking it up. All it needed was a cleaning.

But he didn't need it anymore. He didn't need to dress the part because the part had changed and grown in new directions. He looked at the android standing patiently waiting for him. He thought of Celine going to all the trouble of organizing a party and then buying an android and programming it for a hunt.

"Come on," he said to the android. "We have to hurry. We have a party to get to." The android started trudging along with him again.

"You know, it's being thrown by Celine," Vincent said. "By my niece, Celine."

He and the android walked out of the park. He never looked once looked back for the cape.

Bloody Aversion

Dennis had a problem. He was a vampire.

That wasn't the problem, no. Dennis quite liked being a vampire. He'd always considered himself a night owl, even when he was human. He preferred the darkness to the sun. Being fair-skinned and red haired meant he'd burned easily under sunlight, a condition that only increased once he became a vampire. He was quite used to staying in the shade, so having to avoid the sun altogether wasn't that much of a hardship.

He loved the whole not-aging thing. He'd been turned just as he was starting to get a touch of crow's feet at the corners of his eyes so he could still blend in well with younger people. For a week or two, he flirted with the whole cape look but decided it wasn't for him. Even slicking his hair back, it just looked silly for a red-haired man to be walking around in a cape. He preferred a nice camel brown sportscoat. Gave him a slimmer line.

He'd been happy to discover he didn't need to sleep in a coffin. As long as he was securely out of the sun, it didn't matter where he slept.

But there was one important aspect of being a vampire that caused him no end of trouble and Dennis just didn't know what to do about it.

He hated the sight of blood.

He'd always hated the sight of blood, even as a child. He remembered fainting when his best friend, little Suzy DeMar, had fallen from the swing set and skinned her knee. At first the scrap had been just raw but then the red blood started flowing, trickling down her leg in tiny rivulets... One look had been all it took and Dennis fell over in a dead faint.

It didn't get any better as he got older. He'd had to quit the football team because he couldn't stand seeing any cuts. He skipped biology classes and almost flunked out. For a while, he'd considered being a doctor because he liked to help people but he just couldn't get past the whole blood thing. Becoming an accountant seemed a good way to help people and avoid any bloodshed.

Everything had been fine until, well, becoming a vampire.

Now Dennis found he had a huge problem.

At first his sire, a petite woman named Giselle, looked after him. She brought him a thermos full of blood and he drank it with his eyes closed. But after six months, she became more and more impatient with him. Sometimes the mouth of the thermos had blood dribbling down it and he couldn't take it from her. One night, she pushed it into his hand and smeared blood across his palm.

Dennis felt his vision start to go black, fading around the edges into a narrow tunnel. He stumbled back from Giselle, not taking the thermos but she'd already let go and it fell, spraying blood across the tile. Dennis took one look at the red puddle...

He was unconscious before he hit the floor.

He didn't hear Giselle swearing at him in French.

When he woke up, Giselle was sitting by the bay window, smoking one of her foul smelling cigarellos. He sat up, almost afraid to look around but the thermos and puddle of blood were gone. Giselle must have cleaned it up.

His knees popped as he stood up. Giselle's head swiveled toward him and her glare struck him. He almost staggered back from the force of it. The only time he'd ever seen her look so intensely was the night she'd chosen and turned him.

"You have been a huge disappointment, Dennis," she said. "Things can not continue this way."

"I'm sorry," he said. He hung his head. "I don't know what to do. I've never been able to deal with it."

"You're going to have to," she said. "My patience is at the end of the thread. There is no more left. You must find a way to be a full vampire or I'm leaving."

"Giselle, please, give me another chance."

"I have given you plenty of chance. Now I want to see progress. And when I say I will leave, you will not be left behind. I made you and I will unmake you."

"Okay." He held up his hands in surrender. "I'll find a way. I'll be that vampire you're looking for."

Her eyes narrowed through the smoke of cigarello. "Promise?" The question contained equal parts hope and threat.

He swallowed, remembering the strength in those thin arms that pined him down, the intensity of the pain and overwhelming pleasure as she bit into him. He had a feeling an unmaking wouldn't be so pleasant and would definitely end with the end of him.

"I promise," he said.

He began where all good research began, on the Internet. He discovered his fear had a name. Hemophobia, the fear of blood. He tried to read more about it but every time he opened one of the articles, a photo of blood would appear. Several times he almost fainted before he could close the browser windows. This was not helping. If he didn't find a way to deal with this Giselle would make good on her threat. For now, she seemed mollified with his efforts. She returned to the practice of bringing him blood in a thermos but he knew it wouldn't last. He had to take care of this once and for all.

He spent another night searching on the Internet, avoiding photos but soon came to realize he wouldn't be able to deal with this by himself. Sitting in front of a computer wasn't going to help him. And Giselle was starting to look at him with narrowed eyes.

He had to do something else.

He was going to have to see a therapist.

When he mentioned it to Giselle, she didn't laugh the way he expected. A thoughtful look came across her thin face. She nodded.

"Remember to ask if they take evening appointments," she said. "You won't be able to go during the day."

"Right," he said. He returned to the computer and found a list of therapists who dealt with phobias.

His evening appointments-only restriction cut the huge list down to a meager ten. He showed it to Giselle, to prove he was still trying, and also to ask her advice.

"I don't know which to pick," he said. "How do I know which one will be able to help me?"

She puffed on her cigarello. "Try them all. See who you feel most comfortable with."

"Um, there's a problem," he said.

"What is that?"

"I don't have the money for this."

She shook her head. "I pay for it, silly." She stood up from the bench by the window and crossed the room to the large antique desk. She opened the drawer and pulled out a large mahogany box. When she opened it, he saw stacks of money inside.

"How much you need?"

"I don't know."

She tossed him a bundled stack. He caught it and counted. Roughly five thousand in his hands.

"Start with that," she said. "But I expect results."

He nodded. "I promise."

The next evening, he got up right after dusk and started making calls. He discovered five of the therapists were either booked or out of business. That left him with only five options: Wilson, Bromheld, Travers, Higgins and Smithers. He called each in turn, asking for an appointment in the evenings as soon as possible.

Much to his relief, he was able to get appointments with each one over the next two weeks. When he hung up the phone he turned to Giselle and smiled.

"I start with Dr. Wilson tomorrow night," he said.

She nodded. "Good. Let's hope one of them can help you." She slipped her long black coat over her red corset. "I have hunting to do."

She gave him a pointed look.

"I'm going to go out too," he said.

"Fine," she said. "But don't start anything and faint in the middle of it. It's too much of a mess for me to follow up on."

Dennis hung his head as she swept out of the room. With her petite frame and flowing clothes, she was the perfect vampire. She didn't have any problems with blood at all.

Why couldn't he be like that? Why did he have to carry his phobia about blood into his undead state with him? Giselle had explained how the man he was would determine what he would be as a vampire but he didn't have to like it.

Maybe he didn't need therapy. Maybe he could do this on his own.

He grabbed his brown camel sportscoat and headed out himself.

He ended up in a jazz club, standing at the bar, nursing a club soda. He never bothered with alcohol. It had no effect on his vampire chemistry save to give him a bit of a headache and make his mouth taste fuzzy. So he nursed club soda in a short glass, pretending it was vodka.

At the end of the bar, he spotted a cute little brunette. She smiled at him, then looked at the stage where a piano, guitar and drum trio were playing. Dennis focused on her, using the vampire psychic call to coax her to look at him again. Her head tilted then turned. Her big brown eyes widened, as did her smile.

He picked up his glass and moved to the end of the bar.

Now that he was a vampire, it was so much easier picking up women. The whole hypnotizing with the eyes, sending out commands psychically, ensured that even Dennis managed to connect. Sure enough, this lovely brunette (Julia, she told him her name with a laugh), only needed the slightest nudge before she slipped her hand through his arm, willing to follow him anywhere. He led her down the stairs, heading toward the washrooms. He knew she expected him to make love to her but he had something else in mind.

The hallway to the washrooms ended with a large door opening to the alley out back. A sign warned that an alarm would go off if the door was opened but Dennis could tell it was a lie. His vampire senses told him there wasn't anything electrical attached to the door. He grabbed the bar and pushed.

Julia giggled. "Aren't you going to get in trouble?"

He looked back at her, giving her his best sneering smile. "Trouble's my middle name, baby." God, he loved being a vampire. No other way could he ever get away with such a corny line, and while wearing a brown camel sportscoat.

She laughed and followed him through the door.

The back alley was dark and reeked of garbage and urine. Julia's nose wrinkled at the smells until Dennis focused his attention on her. In the dim light from the twenty watt bulb, he could see her eyes defocus. He pulled her farther down the alley, away from the light, then pushed her against the rough brick.

He pressed his body against her. If he'd still been human, feeling her soft curves against him would have definitely aroused him but the only thing that interested him now was the soft curve of her neck. He tilted her head. He could smell the blood underneath her skin. All he had to do was bite and drink. He didn't have to look, he just had to swallow.

He could do this. Then he could tell Giselle.

She would be so proud of him. She wouldn't glare at him again. Instead, she'd look at him with pride, maybe even admiration. After all, he would have conquered his fear. She'd never had to do that. Being a vampire was so easy for her.

He licked Julia's neck, tasting salt and sweat. Beneath him, the woman shivered. He could hear her heart pounding. She was ready. All he had to do was bite. He unsheathed his fangs and pressed his lips to her neck. His teeth pressed against her flesh. He closed his eyes and bit down.

Warm blood gushed into his mouth. He swallowed and swallowed. This was so much better than the thermos! This was fresh, alive. He was doing it! He'd conquered his fear.

His eyes popped open.

He caught sight of her shoulder. Tiny rivulets of blood dribbled down, staining her shirt. Darkness narrowed his vision. His knees wobbled and buckled. His eyes rolled back.

He fainted.

He woke up a few minutes later. His head had landed in a pile of discarded lettuce. He heard the creak of the door open onto the alley and several sets of footsteps piled out.

"There he is, that's the creep who bit me!"

He looked up. Julia stood just outside the back door, pointing at Dennis. Two big burly bouncers from the jazz club started down the alley toward him.

Dennis scrambled to his feet. The left shoulder of his sports coat was soiled. He felt mashed lettuce in his hair. How humiliating! The image of Giselle's admiring glance faded from his mind, replaced by her sneering laughter. She'd never let him forget this disaster. He was never going to be able to feed himself. Giselle would leave him and he'd starve. But vampires didn't die if they starved, they just became more and more skeletal, weaker and weaker until they could barely move.

And all because he couldn't stand the sight of blood. What a pathetic vampire he was!

The two burly men's approach caught his attention. He saw hands the size of large hams reaching for him. They grabbed him by the arms, dragging him into the light. The man on his right raised a huge fist.

Dennis wrenched his arms forward, breaking the men's grips. They yelled and dove after him as he darted down the alley. He didn't need to deal with these two lummoxes. He spun and slashed, hooking his hand so his claws sprang forth. They sliced through the men's cheeks and chests. Dennis turned his head away so he didn't see the splashes of blood.

He ran. The moans and cries of the men

followed him down the alley and echoed in his head all the way home.

He arrived before Giselle, giving him the chance to shower (in the dark so he didn't have to watch the blood from under his nails running down the drain) and clean up his jacket. The soiled mark wouldn't come out so he tossed the jacket. If she asked, he'd tell her he got tired of it.

After tossing out the jacket, he sat in the corner in the dark waiting for Giselle to return.

Looked like he'd be keeping that appointment with the therapist after all.

"How did you find me again?" Dr. Wilson said.

"I need night appointments," Dennis said. "You have them and had an opening tonight."

"Yes, that was fortunate. So tell me, Dennis, why did you come to therapy?"

"I can't stand the sight of blood," Dennis said. "It makes me nauseous and I always faint."

"That's unpleasant," Dr. Wilson said. "Do you work in a profession where you see blood on a regular basis?"

"No, but it's a big problem," Dennis said.

"And why is that?"

Dennis hesitated. Giselle had told him not to tell but Dennis didn't think he'd get anywhere if he wasn't completely honest in therapy. Besides, if Dr. Wilson didn't turn out to be the right doctor, Dennis could just erase the memory using his vampiric psychic abilities.

At least he hoped so.

Dennis took a breath. Now or never.

"I'm a vampire," he said. "Blood is rather an important part of my life. I need to find a way to deal with my aversion."

The pen scribbling on the pad of paper on Dr. Wilson's lap stopped, hovering over the page. "Excuse me," the doctor said. "Did you say you were a vampire?"

"Yes," Dennis said. "It's just been about six months now so I'm very new at it."

"I see." The pen commenced its scribbling. "So this aversion is hampering your new lifestyle quite a bit."

"Yes," Dennis said. "My sire is getting quite annoyed with me. I should be able to take care of myself but she has to hunt for me and bring the blood to me in a thermos." He bowed his head. "I can't even see any blood smeared on the lip of the thermos or I'll faint."

"It does sound like quite a dilemma," Dr. Wilson said.

Dennis nodded. "It is, it really is."

The doctor bent over his pad, making notes. He really did seem interested in helping me, Dennis thought. Maybe this would work, maybe he'd be able to conquer this fear after all. Hope bloomed inside him, filling his chest, making him sit straighter on the couch. If he could conquer this fear, he could look after himself, he could be the vampire Giselle wanted him to be.

He could be the vampire he wanted to be. Images of him sweeping through the city, seducing and draining woman left and right filled his mind. He imagined Giselle waiting for him to return just before dawn. She would lounging in the king-sized bed and when he entered the room, she would stub out that cigerallo and open her arms to him.

All he had to do was get rid of this fear.

"So can you help me, doctor?" Dennis said.

"Yes, Dennis, I think I can," Dr. Wilson said and he smiled.

Dennis beamed back. "Thank you, doctor. Thank you!"

"Tomorrow?" Giselle said. "So soon? Shouldn't you try one of the other doctors first?"

"I felt really comfortable with Dr. Wilson," Dennis said. "I really think he'll be able to help me."

Giselle frowned at the bill in her hand. "He'd better for this price. Okay, you see him tomorrow but try the others too, okay?"

"I don't have an appointment with Dr. Smithers until next week," Dennis said. "Let me just try Wilson for now. Maybe I won't even need Smithers."

"You keep the Smithers appointment anyways," she said, "and we'll see what this Wilson does."

She really didn't have any faith in his judgment, he thought. Good thing he didn't tell her that he'd told Wilson about being a vampire. She would have found a reason to criticize that decision too. He crossed his arms and stared out the window. Sometimes he wished she'd never turned him into a vampire.

The next evening seemed to take forever to arrive, but finally the sun set and it was time for him to go. He didn't really like taking the streetcar, having to smell all those smelly humans, but he didn't have much choice. He'd forgotten Giselle had a gallery opening and couldn't drive him so he was stuck with the streetcar.

He managed to get a window seat and sat watching the lights flicker past the streetcar as they headed east. Dr. Wilson's office was in his house, just a block south of Richmond Avenue. The streetcar stop was just in front of the church at the corner and although Giselle told him it was a myth that the church could hurt vampires, Dennis found himself feeling uneasy as he stepped off the car in front of the steps leading up to the church. He ducked his head as the doors closed behind him. He turned left, shoving his hands in the pockets of his plain black jacket, and hurried down the street. Only when the church was a block behind him did he relax.

But he didn't quite feel like himself. This black jacket was a little too tight across the shoulders. He really missed the brown camel sports coat. Such a shame he'd ruined it. If not for this damnable fear, he would have been able to finish with the girl and not got a speck of dirt on his jacket. Just another reason to deal with it once and for all.

The doctor's two storey house sat back from the street with a nicely tended front lawn. The office section was in the back of the house so Dennis walked up the driveway toward the back door. He hadn't noticed the cars in the driveway last night. One was a large white van. It almost had an ambulance look to it. Maybe the doctor had other patients in the evenings, Dennis thought.

When he pressed the buzzer, the doctor's warm voice bid him enter. The door clicked open and Dennis walked in. When he entered the office, he found Dr. Wilson with two other men. He must be early for his appointment, Dennis thought. He started to back out of the office.

"Sorry, doctor, I thought you were finished. I'll just wait in the waiting area."

"No Dennis, it's all right. Please." Dr. Wilson

advanced on him, holding out his arms. "It's quite all right. You aren't early at all. I was just finishing with these men."

The two wore some kind of dark grey coveralls. They nodded at Dennis as they began to walk past him. Dennis stopped backing away. He moved farther into the office, toward Dr. Wilson.

"I'm glad you could see me again so soon, doctor."

Hands grabbed his arms, pulling them behind his back. Before Dennis could move, they secured something on his wrists, locking them together. The two men grabbed his arms and started pulling him back toward the door.

"Doctor!" Dennis yelled.

"It's for your own good, Dennis," Dr. Wilson said. He followed along behind them as they dragged Dennis out of the house and down the driveway. They aimed for the white van.

"You need more help than I can give you to deal with such a strong delusion as thinking you're a vampire," Dr. Wilson said. "They'll be able to help you at the hospital. Everything will be all right."

The last thing Dennis saw before the door slammed shut was the doctor's nodding head.

With his vampire strength, Dennis almost broke the restraints before the van stopped. When the van stopped, he charged the door but they were ready for him. Four big men piled on top of him, dragging him to a gurney where they strapped him down with thick leather straps. They wheeled him down a long white corridor and stuck him in a small room. They left him still strapped to the gurney, locking the steel door behind them.

Dennis roared his anger and strained against the straps. He could feel them give a little. He would be able to break through at some point but it was going to take time. His appointment had been at nine-thirty. It had to be almost ten-thirty now. Giselle wouldn't return from her gallery opening until almost midnight. He had to get out of here before then.

Yelling wasn't getting him anywhere, so he stopped and saved his strength for twisting of the leather straps. There was one strap holding his chest down. If he was able to turn his head and bend his neck just so... yes, he was able to nibble on the leather. He extended his fangs for greater reach. The flavour was like chewing on an old shoe. Blood definitely tasted better than this.

One more bite and the strap split. He sat up. Now he was able to bend over toward the arm straps. A few moments of gnawing and his right hand was free. He then unstrapped his left hand and his legs. He jumped off the gurney and crossed to the door.

A tiny barred window was set in the steel. Even with all his vampire strength the handle wouldn't turn. He would have to find another way through the door.

All he could hear was the pounding of his own heart. Okay, relax, Dennis, think. There had to be a way out of this, one that wouldn't involve Giselle finding out.

He did a few moments of deep breathing to relax himself. As his heart rate settled down, he noticed the sound of another nearby. In the hallway. Coming closer. He looked through the barred window and spotted a nurse approaching.

He focused on her with all his vampire

attention. The crisp, short steps faltered. They slowed and then stopped. Right outside his window, a pair of brown eyes looked at him, a glazed, vacant expression in them.

"Open the door," Dennis said. He hadn't learned how to give complex commands without speaking yet. Giselle was going to teach him once he was able to hunt on his own.

"I... I don't have a key," the nurse said.

Dennis stared deep into her eyes, implanting his will as strongly in her mind as he could. "Get the keys to the door and bring them here." He didn't want to get any more complicated than that. The simpler the commands the better.

She hesitated and then turned away. He listened to her rubber shoes hiss against the tile as she walked back down the corridor. He clenched his hand together. Had it worked? Should he start looking for another way out? A quick glance around his cell showed him there wasn't even any ventilation in the ceiling for him to climb through. The only way in and out was through this door.

He waited. And waited.

Finally he heard the hiss of her shoes on the way back. He peered around the edge of the window. Her hand carrying the key was the first part of her to appear. His heart pounded as she stopped in front of the door, waiting for further orders.

It had worked! He'd never sent someone off with a command and had them return. He took a deep breath to settle his excitement. He had to concentrate; he still needed to get out of here.

He pressed his face to the window, capturing her gaze again.

"Put the key in the lock and unlock the door."

She hesitated. He was now pushing against an inhibition about releasing a patient. He focused his will. Come on, come on! Her hand jerked forward. Stopped. Then jerked again.

In short bursts of movement, her hand moved toward the lock. Dennis felt sweat bead on his forehead from his efforts to concentrate. Every part of his body tightened. His neck ached.

Her hand shoved the key into the lock and turned.

"Open the door," he told her.

Now that he'd broken through the one

inhibition, it was easier to break the others. Her hand grabbed the door handle and pulled. The door seemed to hiss as it swung open.

Dennis sagged as he let his concentrate lapse a little. He stepped into the corridor. The nurse stood with her hand on the door. He took her hand and led her inside the cell.

"Sorry about this," he said and closed the door on her.

He grabbed the key and headed back down the corridor.

Finding the exit wasn't too difficult. He snagged the attention of the first security guard he found and had the man escort him out. Just before he left, he hesitated with the guard. If only he didn't have his aversion, he could feed off the man. Of course, if he hadn't had the aversion he wouldn't have been locked in there in the first place. He released the guard's attention as removing his memories then turned to leave the hospital.

Now to deal with Dr. Wilson.

By one o'clock, he reached the doctor's house

again. This time no vans were parked in the driveway. The neighbourhood was quiet and dark. Dennis went around the back and into the office area. The flimsy door separating it from the rest of the house proved no match for Dennis. Soon he found himself in the doctor's bedroom, loaming over the bed of the doctor and his wife.

He slapped his hand over the doctor's mouth, his nails digging into the man's cheeks. Dr. Wilson's eyes flew open. A muffled squeak came from him.

"Quiet, doctor, we don't want to wake your wife."

Dennis dragged the doctor from the bed and then into the corridor. With a push, he tossed the man down the stairs. The doctor stumbled, grabbing the hand rail as he skidded down. He arrested his fall halfway down and then scurried backward the rest of the way. Dennis followed, flexing his hands, his claws sheathing and unsheathing over and over.

They faced each other in the living room. Dennis punched on the light by the door. The doctor wore flannel pyjamas and looked decidedly undoctorish.

"You tried to lock me away," Dennis said.

"It's for your own good, Dennis," the doctor said. "Your delusion of being a vampire..."

"It's not a delusion." Dennis bared his teeth. His fangs clicked into place. He lifted his hands and revealed his claws.

Even in the dim light he could see the doctor pale. His mouth dropped open as his eyes widened.

"Ahh," he said.

"I am a vampire, doctor," Dennis said. "And just because I'm afraid of blood that doesn't mean I won't kill you."

"No, please," Dr. Wilson said. "I can help you. I swear!"

Dennis narrowed his eyes. "How can I trust you now?"

"I didn't realize, I thought you were delusional." The doctor's words sputtered out fast. "But I can help you with your phobia."

"Prove it."

"Of course, please sit. Sit."

He directed Dennis to the couch while he took the facing arm chair.

"Fainting is actually a survival mechanism," the doctor said. "It's caused by a sudden drop in blood pressure. You see the blood, your blood pressure drops and that causes a fainting spell. One of the ways to short circuit the fainting is to practice tightening the muscles as a way to increase your blood pressure. We can practice it a little."

Dennis nodded. "Okay."

For the next several hours, they practiced. First the doctor showed him pictures of the colour red and instructed him on how to tense his muscles. Then they moved to drawing of blood. They didn't bother Dennis so much and he dutifully practiced the tightening of his muscles, focusing on this quadriceps and his back. The bigger muscle groups, as the doctor said, where you get more bang for your buck. Then they moved onto photos of blood.

The images swan in front of Dennis's eyes.

"Tense up, tense up," the doctor said.

Dennis could feel himself become light-headed. He clenched his fists and squeezed his legs. His back tightened up. After a moment, the light-headedness went away. He breathed deep as the doctor had taught him. The panicked thudding of his heart slowed.

"Excellent," Dr. Wilson said. "Excellent work. That's enough for tonight."

"Wait, I want us to finish."

"We can't do it all in one night," the doctor said. "Come back tomorrow and we'll continue. For now I want you to practice with the picture." He slipped the photo of blood into an envelope and handed it to Dennis.

"You aren't going to try to get me committed again, are you?" Dennis said.

"No, I won't," Dr. Wilson said.

"And I don't want to see any anti-vampire stuff around here," Dennis said. "I'll be very angry."

"You won't," the doctor promised.

"Okay. I'll take your bill then."

"Let's leave that for now," the doctor said. "We can discuss payment after. Come back tomorrow night around ten, after my other patients."

He ushered Dennis out the door and waved him goodbye.

Giselle eyes him suspiciously when he returned. "Why are you so late?"

"The doctor wanted to practice and make sure I was doing it right."

He told her about the drop in blood pressure and tensing of muscles. Then he showed her with the photo of blood. The image made him sway on his feet until he tensed up enough and practiced the deep breathing. Giselle nodded and a smile spread across her face.

"Good, Denni, good! Soon you hunt on your own, nes'pa?" She kissed his cheek.

He relaxed, relieved that he didn't have to tell her how he'd confessed to the doctor and then been locked up.

Finally it was going his way.

He practiced for the rest of the night and even through the morning in their darkened bedroom. Finally Giselle's sleepy voice complaining drew him back to bed and he slept through the afternoon. The next evening he prepared to return to the doctor's office for more practice.

For the next three nights, Dennis returned to Dr. Wilson and practiced with different photos of blood. Always at first glance, he felt the familiar swooning before he tensed his back and legs muscles. Then the deep breaths slowed his pounding heart. He learned to count to ten and release the tension. If needed, he could tense up again to raise his blood pressure but more and more often he didn't need it. Excitement coursed through him. It was working!

Then he had to move onto the real thing.

"Ready, Dennis?" Dr. Wilson set a white plate on the table.

Dennis nodded. "I'm ready."

The doctor turned his back, blocking Dennis's vision of the plate. When he stepped back, he'd dribbled red water onto the plate. Dennis practiced his technique even though the water didn't bother him.

The doctor used a tissue to clean up the plate. "One more time."

He blocked the view of the plate, then stepped aside. This time, a thick red puddle spread across the middle of the plate. Blood!

Dennis felt his vision narrow. His heart thudded in his ears. He swayed on his feet.

"Tighten, Dennis, tighten!" A voice called to him.

Dennis tensed his legs and his back. He clenched his fists. After a moment, he remembered to breath deep. The tunnel vision began to dissipate. He counted to ten and released. The tunnel started to darken so he tightened up again and took another deep breath. This time when he released it, he felt steady.

He stayed upright. He stayed awake.

Dr. Wilson applauded.

Flush with victory, they tried it several more times. Each time, Dennis had to tense up at least twice. He frowned but the doctor told him not to be so impatient. They'd made excellent progress.

Even Giselle seemed to think so when he told her about it that night.

"This is wonderful, Denni!" She clapped her hands together. "I am so proud of you!" She threw her arms around his neck and kissed him on both cheeks, European-style.

He thought he felt blood warm his pale cheeks. Was he actually blushing? Giselle's delighted laugh told him he was. He gave a bashful smile.

"Soon we will hunt together," Giselle said. "It will be like I dreamed. Oh Denni!"

That day she lay curled up against him for the whole day. He felt so euphoric he barely slept a wink.

The next night he hurried to Dr. Wilson's office, eager to build on his victories. He found the doctor sitting behind his desk, his hands folded over a manilla folder.

"What next?" Dennis said. "Do we keep practicing?"

"Not so fast, Dennis," Dr. Wilson said. "Have a seat, I want to talk to you about payment."

"The cheque is good," Dennis said. "I'm quite sure it is."

"This isn't about money," the doctor said. "I want something else in exchange for helping you."

Unease twisted Dennis's stomach. He suspected where this might be going and he didn't like the direction. "Oh?"

The doctor nodded. Dennis recognized the eager gleam in his eye. "I want you to make me a vampire. I want eternal life."

Dennis shook his head. Giselle had explained to him that he wouldn't be able to turn anyone for at least five years. It took that long for all the enzymes or whatever to replicate through his entire system. Any one he tried to turn before then would die a horrible death, caught halfway between human and vampire.

"It's not possible for me to do that now, doctor," Dennis said. "In five years..."

"I don't have five years," the doctor said. "I've got lung cancer and they tell me I'll be dead within the year. You can stop that."

"I can't," Dennis said. "I'm sorry, Dr. Wilson. I'm not able to turn anyone for at least five years."

The doctor shook his head. "What are you talking about?"

"I don't understand the whole biology of it but I'm just not able to yet. I wish I could help you."

Dr. Wilson's hand tightened on the folder. His knuckles turned white.

"I'm not doing any more for you unless you turn me. Or get your sire to do it. Until then, the treatment is over."

He pushed back from the desk and stalked across the room to the door leading to the house. As he crossed the threshold, Dennis saw strings of garlic hanging there. He'd vampire-proofed his house!

Dennis left the doctor's office in a panic. What could he do? If he confessed to Giselle that he'd told the doctor about being a vampire she would be furious. He'd broken the code of secrecy and she would be within her rights to put him down. But if he stopped treatment now, he might never get better. Even with those other doctors, what were the odds that they would have such rapport?

Maybe he'd learned enough of how to control his reaction. Maybe he could go the rest of the way on his own. There was only one way to find out.

He headed for the alleys near the docks. Lots of homeless or drunk young men passed out in the alleys there. He'd be able to test his new resolve.

Sure enough, he found a young man slumped in the alley outback of one of the pubs. He sat propped up against a dumpster but it was dark enough that no one would notice Dennis bending over the man.

Dennis didn't want to risk waking the man so he lifted the man's arm. A tattoo of a ship decorated the inside of his forearm. Dennis aimed for just below the man's elbow. His teeth sank into the smooth flesh with ease. Warm blood flooded his mouth. He swallowed and swallowed. He was doing it! He was feeding for himself!

Tiny dribbles of blood flowed down the man's arm, covering the ship. Tunnel vision began to darken for Dennis. Crouched as he was he found it difficult to tense his muscles and continue feeding. He released the man's arm. Now more blood smeared across it, more than Dennis had ever practiced with. He felt his heart pounding in panic. His vision darkened...

He managed to push away and stagger down the alley. Sagging against the wall, he practiced his deep breathing and muscle tensing. After five minutes, the panic attack faded.

At least he hadn't fainted. He supposed that was one positive.

But he wasn't any closer to overcoming his phobia.

No matter how he looked at it, he was going to have to return to Dr. Wilson, and find a way to make him a vampire.

"Do you understand my terms?" Dennis said. "Until you fix me, I'm not doing it."

"Yes, I understand," Dr. Wilson said. "But I need some assurance from you. I just can't take your word for it."

Dennis pulled out a silver chain with a strange engraved medallion. "This will prepare you for the change. Wear it against your skin and the magical properties will begin to work on you."

Dr. Wilson took the medallion and slipped it over his head. Dennis watched as the medallion disappeared under the man's shirt.

"Let's get started again, shall we?" Dr. Wilson said.

It took another full month of practice and talk therapy for Dennis to completely conquer his phobia. In that time, he learned he'd been exposed to blood as a small boy and seen his mother overreact, causing him to associate total fear to blood. But now that he needed it, he had to break the link. With this insight and practice, he found his fear draining away, replaced by a growing confidence that even Giselle approved of.

One night after therapy, Giselle met him on the way home. She slipped her arm through his, steering him away from the bus back to their apartment.

"I think you are ready to try real hunting," she said. "Enough of this practice sessions. Then you be finish with this doctor for good."

"Well, not quite for good yet," Dennis said.

Giselle looked puzzled. "Why, Denni?"

He looked away, embarrassed. "I made a promise."

"What promise?"

"I said I would turn him into a vampire. He's got lung cancer."

Giselle dropped his arm and stomped her foot. "You told him about us? You can not make such a promise! You can not turn anyone."

"I know, I told him that but he said it was the only way he'd help me."

Giselle's eyes narrowed. "So why did he help you?"

"I gave him a medallion. Told him it would prepare him for the change."

"What medallion?"

Dennis shrugged. "Just some piece of crap I found at a junk shop. He's been wearing it the whole time. But I feel bad lying to him."

"Too bad," Giselle said. "You make a stupid promise. Now we have to finish him off. We can not leave him running and telling everyone about us. Other vampires hear of it and we will be laughing stocks."

She turned and stormed away, her hair bouncing in a bob on her head. Dennis hurried after her. He knew what she was saying was true, they had to deal with the doctor, but he'd come to like Dr. Wilson.

"Maybe we can wipe his mind," Dennis said as he caught up to her.

"Not possible," she said. "You have seen him too many times. Impossible to make him forget all of it. No, he must die and you must drink him. That is your test."

She grabbed his arm, her nails pinching his skin. "You had better pass this, Denni."

They reached the doctor's house and Dennis led her to the back office. Although Dennis had been Dr. Wilson's last appointment, Dennis could see the light still on inside. Dr. Wilson was probably finishing up his files. Dennis knocked on the door.

Footsteps approached and Dr. Wilson pulled the door open. Surprised lighted his face. "Dennis! What's wrong? Why are you back?"

"I wanted to introduce you to Giselle, doctor," Dennis said.

"Oh, come in then." Dr. Wilson stepped back and allowed them entrance.

Giselle slipped past and into the far corner of the room. Dennis saw her eyes glinting as she tipped her head. The doctor closed the door and Dennis could almost hear her voice saying, do it.

"It's a real honour to meet you, Giselle," the doctor said. "Dennis has told me so much about you."

"Charmed," Giselle said, extending her hand. She glared across at Dennis.

"Was it difficult for you?" Dr. Wilson said. "Being the only girl in your family? Having your brothers all die from the plague and your father accusing you of witchcraft?"

"How do you know this?" she said.

"Dennis told me a little bit about your background," Dr. Wilson said. "That must have been a terrible betrayal."

She looked uncertain. "I suppose."

Dr. Wilson sat down on his armchair and gestured toward the couch. "Why don't you tell me about it?"

"There is nothing to tell," she said but she moved to stand in front of the couch.

"Do you forgive your father?"

"Forgive him?" Her voice rose in a shout. "How can I forgive him? He disowned me and cast me into the street. This is what happened to me!" She spread her arms.

Dr. Wilson nodded to Dennis. "Could you wait for us outside, Dennis? I think Giselle deserves some privacy."

"Of course, doctor."

Dennis closed the door behind him.

Even vampires deserved to be well adjusted and once Giselle realized that, Dennis knew she would come around. After all, there were a lot of vampires with problems out there. A doctor with full night hours could help a lot.

That medallion might end up working for Dr. Wilson after all.

The Whitest Smile

Wilbur Morris loved being a dentist. Unfortunately no one loved him as a dentist.

Trying to accommodate patients, Wilbur stayed open late three nights a week but still barely managed to fill the time slots. Even as he offered to stay open later, his clients continued to drift away, as if they knew his practice was in dire trouble. In desperation,

Wilbur offered a special half off any treatment on Friday evenings from seven to ten.

No one took him up on the offer.

You have to admit failure, Wilbur, old boy, he thought as he dragged the sandwich board notice inside from the sidewalk. He tucked it in behind the receptionist desk. The desk he no longer needed. Why bother hiring a full time receptionist when hardly anyone called?

Switching off the front light, he headed to the back, passing the two examination rooms. He paused in the doorway of each one. Instruments gleamed on the sterile trays. The drills folded neat beside the arm rests. Even the spit sinks and cups were polished. Wilbur believed in a clean, ordered office.

How could it have all gone so wrong?

He didn't overcharge. If anything, his prices were too reasonable. Below guidelines. He didn't believe in being greedy. He wanted to help people, believed he was offering excellent service at reasonable rates. He didn't understand why it wasn't working.

Maybe I shouldn't be a dentist, he thought.

Maybe his mother was right and he should have been a lawyer.

But he loved being a dentist.

He loved the bright, cleanness of sparkling teeth. He loved helping to improve people's smiles. When people had better smiles, their lives went better. They weren't afraid to talk or smile. Misunderstandings cleared away as folks originally thought of as sullen and unfriendly but only afraid of opening their mouths now spoke with confidence and connected with their neighbours. Wilbur had seen the effect, seen the confidence and happiness blossom in people who gained brighter and whiter smiles.

So why didn't they come to him?

"I'm a nice guy," he said to the empty examination room. No one contradicted him. But no one agreed either.

He switched off the lights and headed for the back to pick up his coat. How much longer could he afford to keep the office? He'd known it was a risk leaving the group practice in Lensville to return to the city. He'd expected it to take time, to have some competition in the larger city but he hadn't expected such a complete lack of interest.

Were there that many dentists here? Weren't there enough people to accommodate one more?

It certainly didn't seem that way.

As Wilbur pulled his beige overcoat from the wooden hanger, he heard the tinkle of the front door bell. Hadn't he locked the front door after bringing in the sign? He tried to remember but couldn't. It was such an automatic action, he never paid attention. The bell stopped. Had he actually heard it? Maybe it was wishful thinking.

Or maybe it was someone trying to rob the place.

There wasn't any cash but Wilbur couldn't afford to have the machines damaged. Most of them were leased and although covered by insurance, if he'd left the door open, it would void any claim. Having to pay for those machines would spell the end of his practice.

Wilbur grabbed the black umbrella from the stand by the door. A healthy whack with the heavy wooden handle might give some thief pause, he thought. And if they had a gun? Wilbur pushed that out of his mind. He had expensive dental equipment to think of.

His rubber soled shoes made no sound as he crept back along the darkened hallway. Even with the dim light from the streetlights out front, he could see well enough. Thank goodness, he'd gone for the lighter cream shade on the walls when he'd repainted the offices. It helped reflect more of the light. Unfortunately it would also help the thief.

Wilbur passed the back examination room. He paused just outside the doorway. Turn on the light or not? It would blind the thief but would also blind Wilbur as well. Maybe if he closed his eyes, then squinted. That might work. He gave himself a nod and reached for the light switch.

Even behind his closed eyelids, the light flared. He squinted, gripping the umbrella. The room was empty. He snapped the light off again, plunging back into darkness. The front examination room lay a few paces away. Would the thief have noticed the flash of light on and off? Maybe he would think it was automated.

Wilbur might still catch him.

Gripping the umbrella tighter, he moved toward the front examination room. With each silent step, his heart thudded louder in his chest.

It drowned out everything; the cars driving past on the street out front, the quiet squish of his shoes as they pressed on the white tiles. Could the thief hear his heart? It roared like thunder in Wilbur's ears. His hands trembled as he clenched the umbrella. His knees felt weak.

Replacement costs, he thought, think about the deductible.

Another step and he reached the doorway. His hand fumbled for the light. He closed his eyes.

The light flared. A howling snare sounded. He heard the crash of an instrument tray hitting the floor, the tinkling of instruments sprayed across the tiles. His eyes squinted. He swung the umbrella.

Something hit him on the left shoulder before he could complete the swing. Wilbur stumbled and fell. Someone fell on top of him. The snarl sounded loud in his ear. He smelled the stench of decay.

Tooth decay.

A wide open mouth filled his vision. He spotted over developed canines, yellowed with excess plaque, but the worst were the obvious black holes in the back molars.

"You've got horrible cavities," Wilbur said. "And that halitosis is atrocious."

The mouth closed a little and the face drew back. A pale man with sharp features and somewhat bloodshot eyes stared at Wilbur.

"What?" he said.

"I could fill those for you," Wilbur said. "But I think you need a plaque treatment first. Probably several. When was the last time you saw a dentist?"

The man's browed furled. "I don't remember." He spoke with a thick accent that Wilbur couldn't identify.

"That's no good at all," Wilbur said. "I was closing up but I could do an initial treatment right now. Wouldn't take longer than half an hour. Maybe forty-five minutes."

The man's tongue, narrow and pink, poked out, touching the sharp canines. "What kind of initial treatment?"

"We could get rid of some of that plaque to begin with," Wilbur said. "You've got a nice set of teeth. They shouldn't be so yellow. If you'd just let me up."

And that was how Wilbur found himself bent over the man's open mouth. Even after rinsing several times with the strongest mint flavoured rinse Wilbur found the man's halitosis was still strong enough to almost knock Wilbur back.

"When was the last time you flossed?" Wilbur said.

The man closed his mouth as Wilbur leaned back. "Flossed?"

The initial plaque treatment took almost an hour and a half, almost twice as long as Wilbur expected but he'd never seen a case this bad. He didn't believe in scolding patients but this was a special case.

"If you don't take care of your teeth you're going to lose them," he said. "It can cause tremendous health problems down the road and lead to either expensive implants or dentures. But they're never as good as your own teeth. I think we can save them. I'm willing to do my part but I need you to commit to brushing and flossing on a regular basis. What do you say, Mr. Valensor?"

The man sat in the chair, still wearing the dental bib around his neck. He ran his narrow, pink tongue along his teeth.

"They feel so smooth," he said. "You do good job." He nodded. "I let you live."

"That's very kind of you, Mr. Valensor," Wilbur said. "Now what about that flossing?"

"I...I don't know how."

"Let me show you."

Wilbur gave Mr. Valensor a fresh toothbrush and three packages of floss. At the front counter, he switched on the computer to complete the billing.

"Do you have insurance?" Wilbur said.

The man shook his head. Black hair slicked back on his forehead did not move.

"I do take credit cards," Wilbur said. The printer spat out the invoice and Wilbur picked it up. He slid it across the counter and waited for the reaction.

Instead of balking, Mr. Valensor nodded. "You take cash?"

"Uh, sure."

Mr. Valensor pulled out a thin pocket book from the inside of his jacket. He counted out several fifties and finished with a twenty.

Wilbur counted it out. "I don't have any change here."

Mr. Valensor waved his hand. "You keep the change."

"Fine. Let's set up your next appointment." Wilbur opened the appointment calendar on the computer. "I can see you Tuesday at eleven in the morning."

"No daytime appointments," the man said. "Only evening. Late."

"Um, okay. How about next Wednesday at eight?"

"It will be dark then?"

"Yes."

The man nodded. "I'll take it."

Wilbur filled out an appointment card and handed it to Mr. Valensor. As he plucked it from Wilbur's fingers, Wilbur noticed the long, thin nails on Mr. Valensor's hand. He'd never seen a man with nails like that but he made no sign of it. Wilbur didn't judge. He believed in live and let live.

Mr. Valensor headed for the door, then turned just before he reached it.

"You are a good dentist," he said. "I will recommend you to my friends."

"Please do," Wilbur said.

He blinked and the door was swinging shut. Mr. Valensor had vanished. This time Wilbur did remember to lock the front door. He couldn't trust that every thief would turn out to need dental work and be distracted by it.

Little did Wilbur know that he had just saved his practice.

The days still passed with few patients, but by late afternoon the phone began to ring. Men and women with strange accents or deep, gravelly voices asked for evening appointments. Within a few days, Wilbur had filled all of his evenings for two weeks. He tried to talk them into daytime appointments but they all insisted on evenings. The clamor for evening appointments forced him to extend his evening hours. He decided to close in the mornings, letting himself sleep in. Since he had few daytime patients, it didn't matter.

When he asked how they'd heard of him, every one of them mentioned Mr. Valensor.

Wilbur had never been so glad of almost being robbed in his life.

The one thing he did notice about all his new patients was the pallour of their skin and every one of them had the worst halitosis and a terrible build up of plaque. They all confessed to not having seen a dentist for years. Centuries, insisted Mr. Belaossa although he said it with such dramatic flare Wilbur knew he was joking.

They all insisted on paying in cash, pealing off fifties and twenties, never asking for change. Before Wilbur knew it, he was having to make night deposits. He'd never had to make night deposits before. The thought of it made him giddy.

His practice was becoming successful. He'd found his niche.

Then she walked in.

'Mianna Travosa' her appointment card read. Wilbur remembered her voice when she gave her name in a deep, slow whisper. Her skin was as pale as the others but seemed to glow against her long black hair and her black dress. Eyes so dark they appeared black stared at him without blinking. Her face was a multitude of angles, high cheekbones and a slim jawline but rounded enough to be feminine. He held out his hand to show her to the back examination room. Her fingers slipped into his hand and the shock of her cool flesh sent a shiver across his shoulder. Her long pointed nails were painted a deep, dark red.

As she lifted her skirt to sit in the chair, Wilbur hurried to stand behind the head rest, out of her range of vision. His pants felt suddenly tight. How horribly unprofessional of him. He'd never had such a reaction to a patient. He hurried to the sink and turned the water on cold. Dousing his hands, he soaped up and scrubbed the skin hard. After a moment with the freezing water, he felt less restricted and more calm.

He returned to her side and slipped the bib around her neck, managing to avoid more than a passing glance at the way the neckline of her dress plunged down to reveal the swell of her breasts. He clipped the bib in place. She tilted her head, a slight smile curving her full, red lips as if she knew where he'd been looking. Of course, she was a beautiful woman and was used to such attention.

Wilbur blushed as he pulled his mask up onto his face. He was never more glad of having to wear a face mask. He hit the button on the chair and adjusted it down. She lay prone before him, her long fingered hands folded in her lap.

"Please open wide," Wilbur said.

Her halitosis was as bad as the others but the plaque build up was less. From his initial examination, he didn't see any cavities but x-rays might show some smaller ones. Best to catch them early, he always thought. Like all of Mr. Valensor's friends, her canines were quite well developed, sharpened into a point. He completed the initial exam.

"I'd like to take some x-rays," he said. "I don't see any major problems but it's always good to get a baseline. Then I'll get rid of some of that plaque and we can get that halitosis taken care of."

She bowed her head. One hand came up to touch her lips.

"Is my breath that bad?" Her deep voice almost purred the words.

His legs felt weak. Thank goodness he was sitting down.

"It's nothing we can't take care of," he said. "Regular brushing and flossing should clear that up before you know it. If it doesn't, then we can start looking at other options. But let's start with the x-rays."

He placed the lead lined cover over her body

and then adjusted the x-ray beside her right jaw. As he retreated behind the partition, he was grateful for another moment to shift in his pants. They felt restrictive and he wondered if he'd be able to get away with washing his hands in freezing water again. Maybe he should get an ice pack and put it in his front pants pocket.

Get a hold of yourself, Wilbur, he thought. So she was a pretty girl. He was a professional and he had to act like it. She was a patient who needed his help and expertise. Best to keep that at the front of his mind.

The brief respite behind the partition helped him regain his equilibrium when he returned to her side. As he removed the cards from her teeth, her tongue flicked out, licking her lush lips. The tip of it caught his index finger. He felt a shock of electricity race up his finger and arm and head straight to his groin. He forced himself to sit down and take measured breaths.

"Now let's get rid of that plaque, shall we?" he said.

She hummed an agreement. Her throat quivered. He fixated on the smooth paleness of the skin at the base of her throat and along her clavicle. Her head turned toward him. The cool heat of her gaze pressured him to turn his head, just a little, just tilt it so, a little more. The smoothness of her lips brushed the side of his neck, sending another electric shock straight to his groin. He barely managed to stop a groan from escaping his mouth. Her lips pressed against his neck then he felt the cold smoothness of her teeth…

"Mianna!"

Her mouth was gone. Wilbur blinked in surprise. What?

Mr. Valensor stood in the doorway. His white hands curled into fists. His thin frame shook with fury.

"What do you think you're doing?"

Wilbur pulled the corner of his white lab coat over his lap. "I… ah was getting ready to clean her teeth."

Mr. Valensor ignored him and stepped to the other side of the dental chair. "Well?"

"I'm sorry, Boris, he is so warm…"

Mr. Valensor grabbed her arm and yanked her out of the chair. Mianna stumbled before she regained her feet as Mr. Valensor dragged her toward the door.

"Please excuse her," he said. "She is young and stupid. She doesn't understand necessities. You will be compensated for your time, doctor."

"But… her teeth…" Wilbur hurried after them. He reached the front room to find a stack of money piled on the counter and the door swinging shut.

He hadn't even had a chance to finish her cleaning.

He wanted to go after them but he couldn't leave the office open, not with money spread across the counter. He scooped it up without counting and added it to the deposit box. Originally he'd been planning to make a deposit tonight after this final appointment but now he didn't feel like it. He locked the box in the safe under the desk and went to clean up the examination room.

Even under the lingering stench of her halitosis, he could smell the musky undercurrent of her body in the chair. He touched the plastic. It felt cool, like her skin, as if her body left no heat behind.

He sat in his chair to arrange the instruments and found himself leaning over the chair again, as if looking at her slim neck and feeling the cool smoothness of her lips on his neck. Only the uncomfortable constriction of his pants brought him out of it.

For heaven's sake, Wilbur, he thought. You're a dentist. You should be ashamed.

He forced himself to keep thinking that even as the memory of her soft lips haunted him through all the tidying up and all the way home until he forced himself to take a cold shower at one am to banish the thoughts of what he wanted to do to her.

Soon Wilbur found he needed to hire help again. Most receptionists would not work past six o'clock and as his practice continued to grow in the evening hours, such reluctance made him more and more impatient. He was willing to pay top dollar but as soon as six hit, most help was out the door. By offering overtime, he was able to get one receptionist to stay to eight o'clock three nights a week but after the second week, she abruptly quit, saying something about the creepy patients and nightmares.

Wilbur found himself alone again.

He dismissed the receptionist's natterings about nightmares. What did that have to do with work? Never mind that he found himself waking up at three am in a cold sweat on a regular basis, his mind filled with vague images of blood and terror. As he lay back on his clammy sheets, he invariably thought of Mianna and the press of her cool lips against his neck. At least in the privacy of his bedroom he could relieve himself but it did nothing to stop the images from filling his mind. His desire remained unfulfilled.

So Wilbur threw himself into work, and his practice thrived.

Now he found it not worth opening until three o'clock. That gave him time to get ready for the evening appointments. He stayed open later and later, to accommodate more of his evening patients. One particularly nasty molar forced him to stay open until almost midnight. With each passing moment, the man in the chair seemed to inflate with energy. His normal white pallor becoming an almost regular pink. It must be the lights, Wilbur thought. It couldn't have anything to do with the time.

That man, Reynaldo Broisa, tipped Wilbur most generously that night. Although Wilbur appreciated it, he was left with the same feeling of disappointment that haunted him every night.

Every night since Mianna.

She never returned for an appointment and Wilbur knew she needed help. Aside from his fevered dreams, it was the only motive he would admit to in the light of day, or the twilight of evening. Although the plaque build up hadn't been as bad on her teeth, she needed to get it removed and needed to have that halitosis dealt with. As a self-respecting dentist, Wilbur wouldn't have it any other way.

But she did not return. Finally, at Mr. Valensor's next checkup, Wilbur could contain himself no longer.

He handed Mr. Valensor the small cup to rinse. As Mr. Valensor swished water in his mouth and turned to spit in the sink, Wilbur pulled the mask down from his face.

"Mr. Valensor, I was wondering about one of your friends," he said.

Mr. Valensor dabbed his mouth with the edge of his paper bib. "Oh?"

Wilbur took the paper cup from the man's hand and tossed it in the waste basket by the door.

"Yes, I was concerned because I wasn't able to finish the plaque cleaning."

Mr. Valensor's eye brows drew together as he frowned. "Ah."

"Yes," Wilbur said. He suddenly felt nervous under Mr. Valensor's cold stare. His stomach twisted. Sweat trickled down his back. Stop it, he thought, he was only concerned about a patient. Her teeth and health were most important.

Squaring his shoulders, Wilbur faced Mr. Valensor's stare. "Yes, Ms. Travosa needs to have that plaque taken care of," he said. "If not by me, then by another dentist."

"But you would prefer if it were you," Mr. Valensor said.

Wilbur felt his cheeks burn. "Mr. Valensor, I am a dentist. My concern is for my patients and the welfare of their teeth."

"Of course, of course," Mr. Valensor said. "Do not trouble yourself with Ms. Travosa. She will be taken care of."

He yanked the bib from around his neck and

climbed out of the chair. Without waiting for Wilbur, he headed back down the hall toward the front of reception area. Wilbur scrambled to catch up. At the front desk, Mr. Valensor stood peeling off fifties to cover the bill.

"What do you mean she'll be taken care of?" Wilbur said.

Mr. Valensor placed the money on the counter and slid it across. His dark eyes seemed to glow with intensity.

"It is none of your concern," he said. "Good night, doctor."

He stared at Wilbur for a moment then turned and left. The door swung closed behind him in its regular slow motion fashion. Wilbur hurried forward and caught the edge before it clicked shut. Before he realized what he was doing, no, before he could talk himself out of it, he stepped outside. The cool evening breeze ruffled his white coat. He locked the door and slipped the keys into his pocket.

Mr. Valensor had headed west but already Wilbur couldn't see him. No, wait, there, several blocks away he saw a figure drifting in and out of the shadows. That had to be Mr. Valensor. No one else was on the street at ten thirty.

Wilbur wrapped his coat around his body and hurried after the man. What exactly he was doing, he didn't allow himself to consider. He just had to make sure that Mianna's teeth were looked after.

The thought of her set his heart pounding. He slowed down, allowing more distance between himself and Mr. Valensor. Certainly the man wouldn't be able to hear Wilbur's heart pounding from this distance but why take the chance?

He kept pace with the figure, cutting across streets against lights if necessary. The minimal traffic in this neighbourhood at night posed little problem. Wilbur had his office in a busy downtown location that thrived during the business hours but became deserted after dark. Wilbur's footsteps were the only ones he heard. Wilbur's shadow the only one he saw except for the distant figure ahead of him.

The figure turned north.

Wilbur followed.

A greater darkness stretched across the west side of street as Wilbur headed north. Even here on the east side, the building lights were few and scattered. What was it across the street with no lights? Then he saw the double wide driveway leading in and remembered.

The cemetery.

Wilbur watched as the figure ahead of him crossed the street and walked along the driveway into the cemetery. Within moments, the figure disappeared into the deeper darkness.

Wilbur waited for a lone car to drive past before he crossed the street. He reached the driveway and began to walk into the cemetery. He made it past the gates before his feet just stopped.

What are you doing, Wilbur, he thought. Without any lights, he could end up lost in the cemetery until morning, stumbling across graves and flower arrangements. Who knew who was lurking in there? Probably some homeless people who wouldn't think anything of beating him up and leaving him there. He should go back to his office and close up for the night. Head home to his lake front condo.

His empty lake front condo.

It was always empty. Wilbur didn't have many friends. Work took up all of his time, especially now with all of the evening appointments. He had no time for socializing, even if anyone did call him.

Which they never did.

No one ever showed the slightest interest in Wilbur Morris. Except…

Mianna.

His feet started moving again and carried him all the way into the cemetery.

When he passed the mile mark he started to hear voices whispering on the breeze. Or maybe it was homeless men waiting to jump on him. His feet slowed. Maybe it was just the trees rustling, their leaves rubbing and sliding against each other. Rubbing and sliding made him think of Mianna again.

His feet moved forward.

The pavement curved to the left but Wilbur continued straight, stepping onto the grass. It crunched beneath his feet. He felt a gentle sloop moving downward. In the distance, he heard the burble of water flowing in a creek. Over the sound, he heard voices again, closer, off to his right. He crept forward, aware it could still be the faceless homeless people that he feared.

The night was not nearly as black as he'd expected. Ambient light from the surrounding area reflected down from the overcast clouds above. He could make out dark lumps rising from the ground. Tombstones, he realized and then remembered what he was walking on.

Or who.

His shoulders hunched as he pressed his arms to his sides. What the hell was he doing out here in the middle of the night walking over peoples' graves? Had he lost his mind? He looked around and realized he didn't know exactly where he was. Oh great, Wilbur, he thought. How was he going to find the street again?

The voices ahead of him increased in volume. Some kind of argument was going on. His feet started moving again without his permission. Over a slight rise, he thought he saw figures standing in the middle of a cropping of tombstones. Wilbur hunched down behind a large square marker.

"…dangerous to all of us." The words floated

on the air. Wilbur thought he recognized the voice. Could it be Mr. Valensor?

"Is it not my fault," a woman's voice said.

"You are always too impetuous. When will you learn patience?"

"I've had enough of your patience!"

The voice rose to a shout at the end of the sentence, causing Wilbur to hold his breath. He recognized that voice. Mianna!

Growls sounded.

"Not all of us think as you do, Boris!" she said.

The growls grew louder. Then Wilbur heard the sound of something striking out and the thud of a body on the ground. He jumped up and ran forward.

In the centre of a circle of tombstones, Mianna lay on the ground, her hand at her throat. Mr. Valensor bent over her, his head buried in her neck. Without thinking, Wilbur leapt on his back.

"Get off her!"

Mr. Valensor reared up, flexing his shoulders. Wilbur found himself flying backward. He landed against a tombstone and fell in a heap at its base. The wind knocked out of him, he gasped for air.

He grabbed the tombstone and started to pull himself to his feet. A steel vice wrapped around his neck, tightening. He gagged, twisting to look. Mr. Valensor's face filled his vision, expression twisted in anger into something horrible. Wilbur remembered it from that first night.

That first night...

"Stop it, Boris!" "Stop, look who it is!" "It's Doctor Morris."

The voices floated around him, soon drowned out by the pounding of his heart and the roaring of blood in his ears. He tried to suck in air, his mouth gaping like a fish, but nothing came. The vice grip of Mr. Valensor's hand stopped any air. Wilbur's fingers pried and pounded but nothing moved that hand. Finally the voices blurred into a loud buzzing.

He crumpled to the ground. The vice on his neck was gone. Wilbur sucked in air as fast as he could. Soon the roaring of his blood faded. His heart slowed. His neck hurt from Mr. Valensor's grip. Wilbur rubbed at it as he struggled to his feet.

In front of him, Mr. Valensor stood in the middle of a crowd of other people. His fists clenched as he glared back at Wilbur. Beyond him, Wilbur could see Mianna, standing with a hand to her throat. Her pale skin looked luminescent in the darkness, her dark hair a suggestion across her shoulders.

"How did you get here?" Mr. Valensor said.

"He followed you, of course," said Reynaldo Broisa. "You were careless, Boris."

"I am not careless."

"Obviously you are or the dentist would not be here." Reynaldo stepped between them. "It is a shame you are here, Dr. Morris. You should not have found out about us."

Wilbur tried to speak. His sore throat ached. He swallowed then tried again. "You mean found out you're vampires?"

A hush settled on the entire group. He felt their attention rivet onto him with laser focus. He almost took a step back. His foot actually moved before he noticed and stood firm. He couldn't show fear, even as his bowels clenched.

This was what a mouse must feel like cornered by a cat, he thought.

"You think I don't know what you are?" he said. His voice almost squeaked. "It wasn't hard to guess. Wanting appointments after dark, the bad halitosis. I'm not as stupid as you think I am."

"Stupid enough to have followed me." Mr. Valensor stepped forward. The others followed, encircling Wilbur. He began to shiver in the cold. He wasn't afraid, no, he wasn't. Well, maybe terrified.

"So he knows about us." Mianna stepped in front of Mr. Valensor and faced him. The breeze brought the faint musky scent of her body to Wilbur. He inhaled deep.

"He hasn't said anything to anyone, has he?" she said. "He continues to treat us, to help us. Even when he knew. Reynaldo, did he not work on your molars?"

Reynaldo nodded.

"Jasmine, did he not consult on your overbite and give you exercises for your jaw?"

A blond woman on Mianna's left bowed her head in acknowledgement.

"Then do we not owe him to hear him out?" Mianna said. She stepped back, turning toward Wilbur, her hand beckoning him to continue. But Wilbur didn't know what else to say. He knew about them, that was the only thing he'd thought of to mention. He'd always known, from the first day Mr. Valensor had broken into his office. Offering to fix the man's teeth was the only way Wilbur could think of to save his life. Then fixing the others just seemed to flow from there.

"I was afraid not to do it at first," he said. "I thought you would kill me. But then I saw you had problems with your teeth, all the plaque build up, the receding gum lines, the cavities. You need a good dentist just like anyone. I took a vow to help people in need with their teeth. I've done my best for you."

Around him, he felt the intensity of their gaze shift. Dark shadows nodded in agreement but Mr. Valensor scowled.

"He cannot learn about us and live. That is the code."

"Damn your code," Mianna said. "We have to adapt to survive."

"Your adaptations would destroy us!" Mr. Valensor's arm blurred as he struck out at Mianna. She leapt back, his fists passing within a hair's width of her cheek. Mr. Valensor snarled and leapt forward, aiming past Mianna and toward Wilbur.

Wilbur stumbled back, feeling Mr. Valensor's claws rack across his chest. His shirt shredded. Blood beaded on his skin.

Mianna shrieked as she knocked Mr. Valensor aside.

"Run, Wilbur!"

Wilbur staggered to his feet and ran. The grass felt soft and wet under his feet. He slid as much as he ran. In the distance, he saw streetlights and headed for them. Nothing followed, nothing he could hear but he felt a creeping presence flying toward him. His shoulder blades tightened, clenching his back muscles. Rancid breath warmed the back of his neck. He ducked his head, feeling the air move over his hair as if someone had swiped at it.

A howl of rage bellowed out, followed by a different snarl of anger. Something thudded behind him and a cacophony of growls began. A woman's voice cried out.

It sounded like Mianna.

Wilbur wanted to look back, wanted to stop but he couldn't, knew if he did he'd be dead. She given him this gift, a chance to save his life. He didn't have any right to waste it.

He kept running and didn't look back.

His feet smacked on the pavement and the solid footing gave him an extra burst of speed. He raced into the street, not bothering with the light (red) or the crosswalk (dark) and kept going. As he reached the corner and turned east, he heard other footsteps following.

Coming up fast.

Wilbur pushed harder. His lungs burned as he gulped for air. A painful stitch pierced his right side. His heart pounded so fast he thought it would burst through his back and he'd leave it lying on the sidewalk behind him.

The dark storefronts blurred beside him. Ahead he saw the sign for Tony's Pizza Emporium, just three stores before his office. He raced past. His fingers fumbled in his pocket.

He had the key out as he slid up to the door. The footsteps following pounded past Tony's. Wilbur jammed the key in the lock and yanked the door open.

Three running steps carried him through the

reception area to the back hallway. He bypassed the first examination room and headed for the second one. A moment later, the pounding footsteps followed him down the hallway.

The light sprang on in the room. The flash of it blinded Wilbur. He clenched the drill and held it in front of him as he blinked. He felt a presence sweep across the room.

"Boris!" Mianna's scream came from the reception area.

A snarl filled Wilbur's ears. The stench of Mr. Valensor's breath filled Wilbur's face. Not as bad as before, Wilbur thought. His eyes cleared to show him Mr. Valensor's sharp canines, ready to bite.

Wilbur shoved the drill forward.

He grabbed Mr. Valensor's collar and pressed the button. The drill whined. The cloying stench of burning porcelain filled Wilbur's nostrils.

Mr. Valensor shrieked and tried to pull away but Wilbur hung on. The vampire twisted his head, dislodging the drill, but not before Wilbur saw the hole burned into his left incisor.

As the vampire howled, Wilbur grabbed a sample tube from the counter. He cut the top and shoved it into the vampire's mouth. He squeezed hard, sending the clear goo into Mr. Valensor's mouth. Mr. Valensor's hands grabbed Wilbur. His nails dug in, piercing Wilbur's skin. Wilbur hissed but held on to the tube until it finished. Mr. Valensor shoved and Wilbur flew back. He hit the wall and slid down to the floor.

He heard Mr. Valensor coughing, trying to clear his mouth.

Mianna appeared in the doorway. She took a step toward Wilbur.

"Don't let him," Wilbur said. "Keep his mouth shut."

Mianna fell on Mr. Valensor. She grabbed him from behind, trapping his arms to his sides. A gurgle of rage sounded. The vampire twisted, trying to escape but she held on. After five minutes, Wilbur signaled her to let him go.

Mr. Valensor fell to his knees when Mianna released him. His hands dug at his mouth but the goo had hardened, fixing Mr. Valensor's open mouthed snarled for eternity.

"It's brand new," Wilbur said. "The latest in dental fixatives. They're testing it to see if it will replace implants. Personally, I think it's too dangerous. What do you think?"

Mr. Valensor lunged for him again but Wilbur retreated behind the chair, out of reach. Reynaldo and Jasmine entered and grabbed Mr. Valensor's arms.

"It's time to change, Boris," Mianna said. "We can't just go around killing everyone anymore. We want good dental benefits just like anyone else."

Mr. Valensor's gurgled response and flailing arms gave his answer. Mianna nodded to the others. Reynaldo and Jasmine began to drag Mr. Valensor away.

"Reynaldo, I'll want to check that molar in a couple of weeks," Wilbur said.

The big vampire nodded. "I'll make an appointment, doctor."

They hauled Mr. Valensor away. Wilbur heard the front door click shut behind them.

"I apologize for Boris," Mianna said. "And for myself. I was… inappropriate at my last appointment."

"Um, that's all right," Wilbur said.

"I just…" She stepped forward. Her thin hand trailed down his bicep. "I've always been attracted to dentists."

Wilbur swallowed in a dry mouth. "Really?"

She nodded.

"Maybe we can go for a drink sometime," Wilbur said. "But you really need to have that plaque taken care of."

She smiled but her lips remained closed.

"If you got rid of that plaque, you could smile more openly," he said. "I could even give you a whitening treatment."

"You would do that? For me? After everything?"

"Sure," he said. "You need good tooth care too."

This time her smile was larger. She leaned forward and kissed his cheek. The sensual musk of her was drowned out by the rotting stench of her breath.

"Have a seat," Wilbur said. "I've got an extra coat in the closet. Let's get started on those teeth."

Wilbur splashed water on this face and dabbed away the blood from his chest. The clock told him it was already after twelve but he wanted to get started on Mianna's teeth right away. She deserved the best treatment he could give her and the sooner he started the better.

After all, he couldn't wait to have a drink with her.

Wilbur pulled up his mask and bent over Mianna.

"Now open wide," he said.

And she did.

About the Author

Based in Toronto, Canada, Rebecca M. Senese writes horror, science fiction and mystery/crime, often all at once in the same story. Garnering an Honourable Mention in "The Year's Best Science Fiction" and nominated for numerous Aurora Awards, her work has appeared in *Tesseracts 16: Parnassus Unbound, Imaginarium 2012, Tesseracts 15: A Case of Quite Curious Tales, Ride the Moon, TransVersions, Deadbolt Magazine, On Spec, The Vampire's Crypt, Storyteller, Reflection's Edge, Future Syndicate* and *Into the Darkness,* amongst others.

When not serving up tales of the macabre, mysterious or wondrous, she volunteers as a zombie or vampire at haunted attractions in October to stalk and scare all the unsuspecting innocents.

Find Me Online

Website - http://www.RebeccaSenese.com
Twitter - http://twitter.com/RebeccaSenese

www.ingramcontent.com/pod-product-compliance
Lightning Source LLC
Chambersburg PA
CBHW061448210726
48287CB00007B/2412